Amazing to think that her womb carried a new life

A tiny person nestled tightly inside, too small for Nora to feel its movements. Yet someday that baby would grow large enough to hold in her arms, utterly and totally dependent on Nora to shelter, guide and love him or her.

Tears prickled as she remembered the distress on Leo's face when she broke the news. If only he were willing to share this joy with her.

He hadn't dismissed the subject and walked away, despite her willingness to let him. The man had a conscience. She also suspected he had a heart...but for whatever reason, it didn't belong to her.

Dear Reader,

Officer Leo Franco, meet Dr. Nora Kendall.

She's seeking a man to father her baby. He's just looking for a good time. But when you meet at a wedding, sometimes it's hard to avoid getting romantic…

As a writer, I like throwing together an unlikely couple and letting chemistry go to work. Nora's in her midthirties, recovering from a painful divorce and anxious to find the right man so she can have the husband and family she dreams about. Leo's dynamic, sexy, five years younger and focused on getting promoted to detective at the police department. Yet together, they ignite fireworks.

I also enjoy writing about a woman who's physically very different from me, and exploring how she deals with her self-image. Nora is a tall blonde (I'm a short brunette), yet no matter how beautiful other people say she is, she feels awkward and geeky. Getting inside her feelings is like having a chance to live someone else's life and make it come out right. As for falling in love with Leo, well, that isn't hard either! Luckily, my husband of thirty-plus years is a very secure man.

I hope you'll join Nora, Leo and me. At a wedding, of course. Please consider this your invitation.

Best wishes,

Jacqueline Diamond

Officer Daddy
JACQUELINE DIAMOND

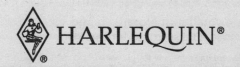

TORONTO • NEW YORK • LONDON
AMSTERDAM • PARIS • SYDNEY • HAMBURG
STOCKHOLM • ATHENS • TOKYO • MILAN • MADRID
PRAGUE • WARSAW • BUDAPEST • AUCKLAND

Recycling programs
for this product may
not exist in your area.

ISBN-13: 978-0-373-75348-2

OFFICER DADDY

Copyright © 2011 by Jackie Hyman

All rights reserved. Except for use in any review, the reproduction or
utilization of this work in whole or in part in any form by any electronic,
mechanical or other means, now known or hereafter invented, including
xerography, photocopying and recording, or in any information storage
or retrieval system, is forbidden without the written permission of the
publisher, Harlequin Enterprises Limited, 225 Duncan Mill Road,
Don Mills, Ontario M3B 3K9, Canada.

This is a work of fiction. Names, characters, places and incidents are
either the product of the author's imagination or are used fictitiously,
and any resemblance to actual persons, living or dead, business
establishments, events or locales is entirely coincidental.

This edition published by arrangement with Harlequin Books S.A.

For questions and comments about the quality of this book
please contact us at Customer_eCare@Harlequin.ca

® and TM are trademarks of the publisher. Trademarks indicated with
® are registered in the United States Patent and Trademark Office, the
Canadian Trade Marks Office and in other countries.

www.eHarlequin.com

Printed in U.S.A.

ABOUT THE AUTHOR

Writing about love and babies never loses its freshness for Jacqueline Diamond, author of more than eighty novels. The daughter of a doctor and a former news reporter who spent a lot of time in police stations, she finds something new in every relationship and every character. Jackie hopes you'll learn more about her and enjoy her writing tips at her website, www.jacquelinediamond.com. If you write Jackie at jdiamondfriends@yahoo.com, she'll be happy to add you to her email list.

Books by Jacqueline Diamond

HARLEQUIN AMERICAN ROMANCE

962—DIAGNOSIS: EXPECTING BOSS'S BABY
971—PRESCRIPTION: MARRY HER IMMEDIATELY
978—PROGNOSIS: A BABY? MAYBE
1046—THE BABY'S BODYGUARD
1075—THE BABY SCHEME
1094—THE POLICE CHIEF'S LADY*
1101—NINE-MONTH SURPRISE*
1109—A FAMILY AT LAST*
1118—DAD BY DEFAULT*
1130—THE DOCTOR + FOUR*
1149—THE DOCTOR'S LITTLE SECRET
1163—DADDY PROTECTOR
1177—TWIN SURPRISE
1209—THE FAMILY NEXT DOOR†
1223—BABY IN WAITING†
1242—MILLION-DOLLAR NANNY†
1273—DOCTOR DADDY
1295—THE WOULD-BE MOMMY**
1320—HIS HIRED BABY**
1335—THE HOLIDAY TRIPLETS**

*Downhome Doctors
†Harmony Circle
**Safe Harbor Medical

Special thanks to Gary Bale
for answering my questions and keeping it real

Chapter One

Dr. Nora Kendall was in no mood for a wedding. Not for mentally reliving her own and not for pasting a smile on her face as she sat through somebody else's, even though she truly wished them well.

Her wedding, which lay five years in the past, had been a stunning ceremony at a hilltop mansion with a couture gown and custom everything. That magical event had been followed by bouquets filling every room on Valentine's Day and diamond jewelry each year as her birthdays advanced toward the mid-thirties. For the holidays, she could always count on tickets to a surprise destination—Paris, Montreal, Fiji, Shanghai.

Talk about your surprise destination. She hadn't seen the divorce coming.

Today's wedding was far simpler than hers. And, in retrospect, probably a lot more heartfelt. Nora had been committed enough, but Reese—well, she still couldn't figure out how she'd failed to see what a louse he was.

She supposed that, given the unhappy memories being stirred up, she should have declined today's invitation. Still, she truly was glad to witness the simple church ceremony between Tony Franco, the staff attorney at Safe Harbor Medical Center where she worked, and Kate Evans.

They gazed deeply into each other's eyes while speaking

their vows. They couldn't stop smiling at each other. They chuckled when Kate's five-year-old son, Brady, dropped the ring as he tried to hand it to his new father, and they kept sneaking loving glances at their baby daughter, cradled in the arms of the best man.

That was Tony's brother, Leo. A police officer, Nora had heard. Or maybe this wasn't really Leo at all, and they'd hired the guy from some casting office in Hollywood, an hour's drive up the freeway. Thick light brown hair, intense gray eyes, the athletic stance of a man who felt completely comfortable in his own body. The best part was the loving way he rocked his infant niece.

The minister broke into her thoughts. Beaming at the gathering, he announced, "It is my honor to present to you Mr. and Mrs. Tony Franco." The guests cheered. Kate and Tony glowed as they nearly skipped down the aisle on their way to a well-deserved happy ending.

Nora might have pretty much given up on expecting one of those for herself, but she still took pleasure in her friends' happiness. At least, she tried to. But did the best man have to pass inches away from her, with the adorable infant gurgling in the crook of his arm? The sweet scent of baby powder twisted Nora's heart with longing.

She must be nuts. She held newborns every day, gently assisting them into the world, reassuring their mothers, sometimes performing life-saving surgery. That was her job and her passion. But there was something about a wedding and a baby that awoke longings she'd tried hard to suppress.

Nora ducked her head to hide her tears.

THE KIDS MADE IT ALL worthwhile for Leo—the uncomfortable suit, the endless posing for photographs and the job of coordinating the bridal party's transportation to the reception at Tony's house.

Brady was a cute little guy, and as for three-month-old Tara, she'd won Leo's adoration from the moment he first saw his niece. He'd been honored when his brother and new sister-in-law asked him to supervise the kids today. Under other circumstances, Kate's sister, Mary Beth, who was matron of honor, would have done kid duty, but she was pregnant and tired easily.

No sooner had they reached Tony and Kate's sprawling, Mediterranean-style house overlooking the harbor than Brady and a couple of cousins dashed to the playroom upstairs. As Leo had hoped, there proved to be plenty of willing volunteers to hold Tara.

That left him free to enjoy the buffet. Being a bachelor uncle gave him the best of both worlds.

All the same, he wished the best man didn't have to stick around to the end. Socializing in a tuxedo wasn't Leo's style. While the guest list included some down-to-earth friends from Kate's days as a hairdresser, there were also far too many smooth-talking doctors, attorneys and city movers and shakers. Exactly the kind of self-centered friends his parents used to cultivate.

Leo was finishing a crab cake when a strong hand clapped him on the back. Good thing he'd emptied his plate or he'd have spilled seafood down a nearby woman's dress.

"Congratulations!" boomed a masculine voice.

"Thanks." Setting the plate aside, he took in the older man's heavy jowls and designer suit, and a name clicked into place. Roy Hightower, real-estate broker and city-council member. His first term many years ago had briefly overlapped Leo's dad's tenure as mayor.

"Your brother has a beautiful home," added Mrs. Hightower, a slender woman he guessed to be in her early fifties but who'd been surgically rejuvenated to a perpetual thirty-something.

"Yes, he does." Leo riffled through his mental catalog for her name. Gina? Jenna? He strove to keep track of such details. In police work you never knew what information might come in handy.

"Are you a lawyer like your brother?" asked Mrs. Hightower.

Leo preferred not to disclose his occupation to people he didn't know well. But then, they were friends of the family. "Police officer."

As the Hightowers absorbed the information, Leo hoped he wouldn't have to field the usual complaints about traffic tickets. A city-council member ought to know that the police didn't make the rules.

Roy cleared his throat. "Here in Safe Harbor?"

Leo gave a nod, but turned that into a head shake at a waiter offering champagne. He limited his alcohol consumption whenever he planned to be driving.

The Hightowers each accepted a glass, and Roy raised his. "Here's to our men and women in blue. The rest of us rely on you to protect our lives and property." It sounded like a campaign speech. Still, Leo appreciated the sentiment.

"What does that mean, exactly—police *officer*?" asked Gina/Jenna. "Is that like a sergeant or a lieutenant?"

The inexact comparison to military ranks confused a lot of people, Leo had learned. "All sworn policemen and women are officers of the law. We're supervised by sergeants, lieutenants and captains. Some large departments have the rank of commander, as well."

"No majors or generals?" Roy joked.

"In Safe Harbor, the only person above a captain is the police chief, as I'm sure you're aware, sir." There. Leo hoped they'd finished with *that* subject. Although he'd been studying for the department's promotional exam to become a detective, he saw no reason to mention his ambitions.

"If you aren't one of those higher ranks, does that mean you're like a private in the army?" asked Mrs. Hightower, her shrill voice carrying above the chatter of the other guests.

People glanced their way. A couple of eyebrows lifted. He could have sworn one woman's nostrils flared in distaste, but that might have been his imagination.

"Sometimes it feels like it," Leo said. "Now, if you'll excuse me, I'm neglecting my responsibilities as best man." With what he hoped passed for a polite smile, he escaped into the throng.

From the dining room, he made his way through other large, open rooms, trying to catch sight of his brother. It was time for the obligatory toasts, and Leo meant to do the family proud. He'd practiced his short speech on his patrol partner, not that she'd been much help. Patty's idea of a major social event was eating bratwurst with her buddies while cheering a football game on TV.

Near the foot of a curving staircase, he saw the blonde he'd noticed at the ceremony. With long hair draped across her shoulders and her green eyes wide, she looked lost and vulnerable, as if she'd wandered into the wrong house, except it seemed unlikely she'd also wandered into the wrong church. Leo was admiring the curves beneath her silky, deep rose dress when her gaze met his.

He caught his breath. She was unbelievably gorgeous. Some rich older guy's trophy wife? But no ring, he noted.

Then she flicked him a mischievous grin, and suddenly she seemed like the girl next door. "Are you *sure* you aren't from Central Casting?"

"Excuse me?" He strolled closer.

She made a face at her champagne glass. "I think I've had too many of these."

"I'm not a waiter, if that's what you were thinking." In

the tux he was wearing, it would be an understandable mistake.

"No, you're the best man. I'm Nora. I work at the medical center."

Obviously, she'd seen him at the wedding, too. Leo didn't usually make slips like that, except around striking, very feminine blondes who seemed in need of a strong shoulder to lean on.

And who, unfortunately, no doubt expected to be showered with gifts and entertained at expensive restaurants. Such had been his experience in a series of disappointing relationships, as Patty was fond of reminding him, usually with an elbow poke to the ribs and raucous laughter at Leo's expense.

Well, his partner wasn't here today. Lucky for him.

"You look beautiful in that dress," he blurted. "I suppose you know that." *Great pickup line, Leo.*

"Oh, I'm not nearly as pretty as people think I am." She blinked. "That didn't come out right."

If she imagined she was anything less than stunning, Leo felt obliged to correct the error. But he didn't get the chance, because a couple in their thirties walked up. A quick mental check turned up the names Kirk and Rosemary Peterson. Rosemary and Kate had met at the obstetrician's office, he recalled. Her husband, who'd been swapping new-father stories with Tony when Leo met him a few weeks ago, was an architect.

"Beautiful wedding," Rosemary told Leo. "You did a fantastic job of keeping the baby quiet during the ceremony."

"My niece has a sweet nature," he replied. "Also, I drugged her."

A free, open laugh burst out of Nora. No giggling behind her hand, Leo was glad to see.

"I've been tempted to do that a few nights myself," Kirk

admitted. To Nora, he explained, "We have a three-month-old son. By the way, I'm Kirk Peterson and this is my wife, Rosemary."

His wife shifted uncomfortably. "Kirk, you remember Dr. Kendall. She's Reese's..."

Dr. Kendall. Well, she *had* said she worked at the hospital.

"Oh, right." Kirk snapped his fingers. "Congratulations. You and Reese must be thrilled."

Nora frowned. "I'm not sure *thrilled* is the word I'd use."

"Hey, we're experts on morning sickness and backaches and all that stuff, but it's worth it," Kirk enthused.

"I beg your pardon?"

Rosemary grabbed her husband's arm. "Honey, Nora is Reese's *ex*-wife. She's not the one who's pregnant."

Understanding dawned on his face. "Oops. Guess I'm a little off base there. Sorry."

Nora didn't answer. Her jaw had dropped. Clearly, she'd had no idea her former husband and his new wife were expecting. Tension snapped through the air like live wires.

Attractive as he found this lady, Leo didn't need a woman still torn up over her divorce. "I'm about to propose a toast. I'll catch you folks later." He seized the chance to make his getaway. The Petersons beat a hasty retreat, as well.

As for Dr. Nora Kendall, she stood stone-still by the stairs, lips quivering. She looked more in need than ever of a shoulder to cry on, Leo thought, and wished he weren't so tempted to offer his.

WHAT A TIME AND PLACE to learn about the ultimate betrayal.

"Babies are great, honey, but don't you see enough of them in the delivery room?" That had been one of Reese's typical answers whenever Nora had reminded him of their longstanding agreement to have a child. Or, "I'd hate to lose the romance in our marriage. Don't you like being able to make love whenever we want? And simply be best friends?"

Best friends didn't cheat and break each other's hearts. Had she been naive, foolish or simply stupid to think a smashingly handsome man with a taste for power could also be faithful and tender till death did them part?

Now Persia was pregnant. An exotic woman with the figure of a fashion model, a face worthy of a magazine cover and a birthday cake with a third fewer candles on it than Nora's, she'd not only stolen her husband but her dreams of a baby, too.

Envy was corrosive, Nora reminded herself. The same went for furious resentment and nasty sarcasm. What did that leave?

She considered a platter of petits fours, chocolate-dipped strawberries and miniature pastries arrayed on an end table. Gluttony, that's what it left.

She had barely reached for a strawberry, though, when the bride, clad in a cocktail dress and clutching baby Tara, whisked down the stairs. "Dr. Kendall! Would you do me a huge favor?" Without waiting for a response, she transferred the infant into Nora's arms. "I was breastfeeding when Tony called to say they're starting the toasts and… Oh, thank you!" Off she rushed.

"Happy to," Nora told the retreating figure. Gingerly, she lifted the infant to her shoulder and inhaled that precious baby scent. It reminded her, strangely, of Leo.

She pictured his leashed power as he'd strolled up the aisle, holding the infant. No wonder she'd felt a spark when he approached a few minutes ago. Too bad the Petersons had interrupted… Good heavens, he'd witnessed that whole awkward scene about Reese. Wouldn't you know it? She'd melted down in front of the first man who'd aroused even a speck of interest since her divorce.

Not much chance of correcting that bad impression. The guy must consider her a basket case.

She was drowning her sorrow in chocolate—not easy while juggling a baby—when she heard Leo's voice echo through the house. "My brother and I haven't always been as close as we are now. It took this wonderful woman, my new sister-in-law, Kate, to bring us together."

Unable to resist seeing him again, Nora followed his mellow baritone into the living room and joined a cheerful throng of the newlyweds' family and friends. By the fireplace stood two tall men, both clad in black-and-white formal wear that put her in mind of a classic James Bond movie. Leo wore a tux with more panache than his brother, in her opinion. Something about him seemed especially sexy to Nora. At least, it did after three glasses of champagne.

"I wasn't too crazy about my first sister-in-law," Leo went on, draping one arm around his brother. "But we won't talk about her today."

Good choice. While Nora had only met Esther a few times, the whole hospital had buzzed when she dumped her husband and her job as a county prosecutor for a high-powered career in the U.S. Attorney's office in Washington, D.C. Not only had Esther refused to take her husband along to share her new life, she'd also abandoned the baby they'd conceived with the help of a surrogate mother. Kate had been only a few months from delivering Tara, who was in fact her own biological child.

Speaking of Tara, she'd just produced a loud burp. Nearby, several guests smiled, while another glared, apparently under the impression that this was some rude visiting baby.

Unfortunately, the burp brought up more than air, and

Nora felt a large wet spot spreading across her shoulder. While she was trying to figure out what to do about it, a grunting sound signaled further action below.

Well, great. Things like this, Nora felt fairly certain, never happened to the exquisite Persia. Although, there might be hope for the future.

Around her, people were raising their glasses. Dimly, Nora realized the toast was reaching its climax.

"…the most dynamic power couple in Safe Harbor, because their power comes from love. To my brother and the wonderful woman he's brought into our family. To Kate and Tony."

Clinking, cheering. Nora would have joined in if she'd had a free hand to hold a glass.

Next to take the floor, or rather, the hearth, was the hospital administrator, Dr. Mark Rayburn, who'd also gotten married recently. "I'll keep this short. Marriage is great and it couldn't happen to two nicer people. To Tony and Kate."

More cheering and clinking. Nora could feel the dampness seeping through her dress and the camisole beneath it. She considered handing the baby to some unsuspecting woman, but her conscience wouldn't allow it.

The next to salute the happy couple was Mark's pediatrician wife, whose advocacy for needy women and children had won her the nickname Fightin' Sam. "Enough of these weak-kneed toasts," announced Dr. Samantha Forrest. "Let's hear it for Kate and Tony. Hip, hip, hooray!"

She led the crowd through two more repetitions of the cheer, each louder than the last. At the climax, the baby started to cry, not a loud wail that might have summoned her parents but a soft hiccupping that wrenched Nora's heart.

"Okay, sweetheart. Let's see where…" She turned, only to find her path blocked by a sturdy masculine body. Shiny black jacket, formal white shirt and, instead of a puny bow tie, a teal necktie that matched the bridal colors. Also, she noticed a hint of darkness beneath the strong line of his jaw where a beard threatened to make its appearance. "You missed a spot when you shaved," she said.

He barely twitched, although anyone else would have felt his jaw. "Is that so? Well, you didn't miss a spot, I'm sorry to say."

"Is it that obvious?" She'd hoped the baby's pudgy little shape would hide the damage.

"I had a great view of the entire proceeding." Leo's nose wrinkled. "Is that what I think it is?"

Around them, people were edging away. "Afraid so."

"Do you know how to change a diaper?" he asked.

"I'm an obstetrician. I think I can figure it out." Technically, that ought to be his job as supervising uncle, but his wary expression indicated he'd do it only if absolutely necessary.

He grinned. "I'm glad you're an expert."

"Where's the changing table?"

"I'll show you." When Leo took her elbow, his large hand seemed to envelope her entire arm. With her knees on the verge of liquefying from all the champagne, Nora appreciated the support.

On the second floor, the chatter of childish voices drifted from a nearby room. When she peeked in, Nora saw Brady and a couple of other boys seated in front of a screen, battling it out on a video game.

"Tony and Kate usually restrict use of the game console, but things are a little relaxed today," Leo told her. Into the playroom, he called, "Hey, guys, did you get something to eat?"

"Yeah!" they chorused, and went on playing.

A loud rumbling seemed to emanate from overhead.

"Their speaker system is kind of powerful," Nora observed as they continued down the hall.

Leo laughed. "That isn't the game. It's raining. Hard."

As if for emphasis, a squall hit the roof with the patter of tiny hailstones. Having grown up in the Southern California town of Santa Barbara a few hours' drive to the north, Nora rarely listened to weather reports, even in February, so she hadn't expected this. "That's fierce."

"It's supposed to taper off soon."

She should have paid attention to those steely clouds on the drive over, and skipped the champagne. An unusually heavy storm could transform low-lying Safe Harbor into an obstacle course of flooded intersections and downed branches. In her current state, she wasn't looking forward to navigating the few miles to her condo.

As she stepped into the nursery, Nora forgot her concern. On the far wall, soft colors created a magical forest, where a shy dragon peered from behind a tree and fairies flitted between the trunks. "How charming."

"Changing table's over there." Leo indicated a chest of drawers topped by a padded surface. Beside it hung a cloth diaper stacker.

If Nora had a nursery, she'd decorate it like this—an enchanting cloudlike mobile above the crib, an old-fashioned rocking chair for soothing a fussy baby and a shelf full of picture books with teddy bears peering out here and there. With a sigh, she laid the baby on the pad and set to work.

Leaning against the wall, Leo watched, his warm expression heightening the bubbly sensation in her veins. "You have slender hands. Very graceful."

What an unusual thing to notice. "A surgeon's hands have to be steady."

"I'll bet you can do a lot of things with those hands," he murmured.

A delicious shiver ran up Nora's spine. She felt suddenly desirable, not at all like a woman who usually clipped back her hair and hid her figure beneath a white coat. Or like a wife whose husband preferred a younger, sexier replacement.

Overhead, another gust of rain hit the roof. The room felt isolated, far from the wedding party downstairs. Intimate and inviting.

She bent to her work. "I deliver a lot of babies with these hands."

"Ever get tired of it?"

"Never."

He loosened his necktie. "Whenever I visit someone at the hospital, I can't seem to resist stopping by the nursery. Those little guys are cute."

"You'll make a great father." When he didn't answer, Nora glanced up to see his mouth twist. "Did I say something wrong?"

"Only that I'm nowhere near ready to be a dad," Leo responded pleasantly. "But I'm game to practice if you are."

His half expectant, half humorous expression stirred a flood of heat. Nora hadn't felt a man's touch in far too long. Was Leo just kidding around or seriously trying to seduce her? And if he was, did she want to take him up on it?

She'd felt a tug of longing from the first moment she saw him. But he was a little too good looking, too quick with a smooth line.

On the table, the baby yawned. "Time for a nap." Carefully, Nora lifted her and moved to the crib. "I guess we should let her parents know she's up here."

"I'll do that," Leo assured her.

She hadn't given him an answer. But he probably didn't expect one, and besides, her soiled dress felt sticky. "I'll go wash my hands and see if I can get out this spot."

"Thanks for handling diaper detail."

"No problem."

When she emerged from the bathroom a few minutes later, she wasn't surprised to find that Leo had disappeared. That was no doubt the last she'd see of him except across a room, Nora reflected with a pang.

Even though she knew perfectly well she'd have regretted yielding to impulse, she wished she could be sure she'd get another chance.

Chapter Two

He hadn't meant to proposition Nora so bluntly. Hard to say why the suggestive remark had slipped from his mouth. Sure, Leo had picked up his share of women under unlikely circumstances before, including once at a fellow officer's wedding. But not…

Not what?

"Not another high-flying blonde," Patty would have said. "Honestly, Leo."

Well, it had come to nothing, anyway. Nora was evidently still dealing with issues from her divorce, and while she'd seemed ripe for a little diversion, she hadn't responded. So he went downstairs before she came back. Best not to push a woman too hard.

Either she wanted him or she didn't. Leo had to admit he wanted her. Okay, given her reference to children, she might have initially mistaken him for husband-father material, but he could deal with that. As long as they both understood from the start that this was strictly a fling, they'd be fine.

He was keenly aware when Nora walked back downstairs that she didn't come in search of him. For the next hour, Leo watched from the corner of his eye as she mingled with her fellow guests, mostly hanging out with Samantha Forrest and a couple of other women from the hospital staff.

Leo didn't try to join them. For one thing, every time he

ran into Dr. Forrest, she tried to talk him into volunteering at a counseling clinic she'd established at the local community center. Teen fathers needed his steadying influence, she insisted. Him, a steadying influence? Obviously, Fightin' Sam hadn't seen the pool table dominating his den.

Late afternoon flowed into evening. At most weddings, the bride and groom quickly headed for their honeymoon destination, but Tony and Kate had decided to delay their trip until Tara was past the breastfeeding stage, so they were lingering with their guests. Although Leo understood the rationale, he didn't entirely approve. If you weren't desperate to rush off to a romantic wedding night, how romantic were you likely to be years later?

Finally, after the ritual serving of the cake, guests began taking their leave. Leo distributed coats and umbrellas and went in search of missing purses, since his normally well-organized brother seemed lost in a cloud of bliss. Good to see the guy had *some* romance in his soul.

Leo also kept track of Nora, who'd snared a corsage to pin over the wet mark on her dress and whose hair was curling in tendrils around her face, a bedroom effect that he found highly appealing. She seemed in no rush to depart, kicking back with shoes off—drawing Leo's attention to her slim legs and shapely feet—while she indulged in more champagne and chocolates.

After a lull, the rain started again, harder than ever. Guests grumbled good-naturedly that they should have gone while they had the chance. Leo agreed. He was tired of being around all these people.

As another batch drifted out, Tony stood in the doorway beside him. "You've been great today. I can't tell you how much we appreciate it."

"Want me to boot out the loiterers?" Leo asked. "I'll bet you guys are ready to crash."

"Oh, they'll go soon enough, now that the food's being cleared. I'll have the caterer pack you some leftovers."

"Great idea."

After his brother wandered off, Leo went into the room where he'd last spotted Nora, but it was empty. No sign of her in the dining or living room, either.

It hadn't occurred to him that she might slip out unnoticed. Not that he'd planned anything, but...

At a rustle on the carpet, he turned. There she stood, bright and glowy, holding her shoes in one hand and her purse in the other. A dark pink bolero jacket mashed the corsage on her shoulder. "Excuse me, sir, are you the doorman?"

He felt absurdly glad to see her. "Yes, ma'am. May I help you?"

"I have a car around somewhere, but there's this awful policeman who might haul me off to the pokey if I try to drive," she said. "Could you call me a cab?"

Did she have any idea how delicious she looked? "What a coincidence. I happen to drive a cab. It's right outside."

She regarded him dubiously. "How do I know you won't overcharge?"

"My customers pay only what they wish," he assured her. "As for the personal valet service, it's free."

"Personal valet service?"

Leo raked her with his gaze. "Removal of dead flowers, part of the standard package. Removal of damaged stockings, on request. Removal of soiled clothing, strictly optional but a lot of fun."

"And here I thought you'd given up," she murmured.

"I never give up."

"How about yes to A, maybe to B and no to C?"

He didn't recall which was which, except that C referred to removing her clothes. Too bad. "I'll be back in a sec."

Leo made short work of leave-taking, and gratefully accepted a carryout box of goodies. Then he dashed out with an umbrella, fetched his car and collected a cheerful, feeling-no-rain Nora at the front door.

"You don't drink very often, do you?" he asked as she slid into the front of his red two-seater. Torrents of water splashed across the windshield and drummed on the roof.

"What gives you that idea?" Tossing her gear atop the junk in the back, she fumbled with her seat belt, got it stuck halfway and meekly allowed Leo to finish the job. Since the task involved stretching it across her rounded breasts, he took as long as possible.

"If you'd expected to drink this much, you'd have arranged to come with a friend," he pointed out, his face close to hers.

"I wouldn't trust my friends to drive in this weather."

"But you trust me?" Another few inches and their lips would meet.

"Sirens shrieking, wheels cutting around the corner in pursuit of evil wherever it may strike," she declared. "You're a pro."

As the belt clicked into place, he brushed his mouth across hers. Mmm. She tasted of chocolate and her lips parted tantalizingly. Then, abruptly, she ducked her head. "We're a little old to make out in public, don't you think?"

"I'd much rather neck in private." He shifted behind the wheel. "Where to, madame?"

She stretched her legs and wiggled her stocking-clad toes. "Harbor Bluff Drive West. The new condo development."

Leo had cruised past there plenty of times on patrol. "Swank place."

"Bought it with my divorce settlement," she said.

He didn't want to discuss her divorce, or her ex-husband or how much money she did or didn't have. He was too busy thinking about that kiss and, at the same time, navigating away from Tony's home. The downpour distorted oncoming headlights and blurred stop signs, and while Leo had no trouble handling the situation, he wasn't so confident about the other motorists.

"What's that wonderful smell?" Nora asked.

No one had ever complimented his car's odor. Ah, the food. "Buffet leftovers. I'm willing to share."

"Clever way to snag an invitation inside."

"You already gave me one."

"I did?"

"When you said yes to B and C."

She contemplated this notion for the length of a red light. "Which one was C?" she asked as they pulled forward.

"Peeling off your dress."

"No, I'm sure it wasn't."

"I'm no good at multiple choice," Leo replied. "I usually check All of the Above. How's that sound?"

"Including my dress? Sorry." Leaning back, she let her eyes drift shut.

Just what he needed, for her to fall asleep. Leo wasn't in the habit of taking advantage of women. Whatever he and Nora chose to enjoy, it had to be by mutual consent. *Informed* mutual consent. Which meant she must be awake and reasonably alert.

He hoped she had plenty of coffee.

The complex where she lived stood atop coastal bluffs. It overlooked the beach and, to the east, the curve of marina from which the town of Safe Harbor took its name. After inserting a key card into the parking lot gate, she pointed the way to her reserved, covered space.

"I live right upstairs, but we have to go around the buildings," she told him as they got out. Not far off, the surf murmured in a gentle background rhythm.

"You planning to put on your shoes anytime soon?" He didn't understand why she was still walking around in her stockings.

"They'll be ruined."

"Suit yourself. Hang on a minute." He grabbed the caterer's box along with a canvas bag that held a change of clothing. "I did promise you food."

"So you did."

Recipe for a wet journey: one umbrella, a bag, a box and two people, one of whom kept zigging and zagging and breaking into song. Specifically, "It Never Rains in Southern California." After a few grumpy moments, Leo realized his tux couldn't get much wetter anyway, and joined in the chorus.

He couldn't recall the last time he'd sung in the rain. Maybe never.

They circled the parking area and proceeded up a walkway, past stucco units with water overflowing the balcony flower boxes. After a little key action, they burst through Nora's front door and paused on a half circle of tile at the edge of the carpeted main room.

Leo's gaze swept the low couches and bookcases artfully placed to divide the large rectangular space into sections for entertainment, relaxing and dining. The soft swirl of grays, greens and corals made him wonder if they'd splashed their way into a tropical lagoon. "Nice."

Nora giggled. "Take off your shoes, flatfoot."

Now, there was an old-timey term that implied a taste for classic movies. She liked other classics, too, he saw from the books overflowing the shelves. As for those couches, he could imagine some *very* classic uses for them. "Yes, ma'am."

Leo discovered his socks were thoroughly soaked, so he removed them, too. The better to enjoy the thick plush of the carpet as the two of them staggered to the kitchen to unload their gear. He put the leftovers in the fridge, and hoped he'd be around to enjoy them for breakfast.

"So what do you do for kicks on a Saturday night?" he asked.

"This," said Nora, and wrapped her arms around him.

He hadn't expected such boldness. But Leo, as befitted a former Boy Scout, was prepared.

They swayed together to silent music that vibrated through him. Leo slipped in the suave moves that women appreciated—cupping Nora's face, studying her for a moment before kissing her deeply—but soon he was swept up by her insistent, mounting rhythm.

He managed to get through A and B, possibly C, if you counted his tie. Since Nora peeled off her own shredded pantyhose, he decided he could safely include removing her jacket among his standard package services. And naturally she needed help unzipping her dress, although she seemed to have no trouble undoing his pants.

He was hot all over, hotter than he'd been since his lusty teenage years. Nearly out of control. Barely sentient enough to mutter, "Are you sure about this?"

In response, she traced her tongue down his chest, which at this point was bare, although he didn't recall taking off his shirt. He was leaning against the kitchen counter with this gorgeous blond vision tantalizing him in ways he'd only fantasized about.

If that didn't amount to informed consent, what did?

With a supreme effort, Leo rallied to lift her dress over her head and toss it aside. Oh, man, he loved the impression of pink lace underthings against pale skin, and then one of them—he was almost certain it was Nora—unfastened her bra and he discovered that she was pink all over.

As he relished her breasts with his mouth, a couple of

vague notions fleeted through Leo's mind. The first had to do with a bed, but why bother when he could simply lift her onto a nearby piece of furniture that resembled an old-fashioned casting couch? Some Hollywood genius must have designed this thing with angles just perfect for what nature intended.

As for the second vague notion, he couldn't remember what it was.

"I think we ought to…" Nora didn't finish the sentence, possibly because he was removing the lacy wisp that passed for panties.

"Hold that thought," Leo advised, and slowly, with a wonderfully mind-blowing sensation, penetrated her softness.

After that, he couldn't think about anything except her.

SHE, NORA KENDALL, NEVER did this sort of thing. But tonight she felt utterly free and completely feminine for the first time in more than a year. Sexy. Young. And a touch delirious.

With Leo, she didn't have to worry about expectations or anything but the moment. He'd offered sex, and she was taking it. Nothing more than that, and thank goodness. He was the most handsome, virile male she'd ever made love with…and she was going to stop thinking about what they were doing and simply go with her sensations right now.

His lips on her nipples…his hardness inside her…his rapid breathing and groans of pure pleasure drove Nora to one shuddering climax after another. She hadn't realized she was capable of this. She sought more, until the power of his thrusts drove them both into another world.

His shout of joy startled her. Reese had never abandoned himself this way. Never lifted her to this level, either.

To hell with Reese. Who had he been, exactly?

"Oh, honey," Leo murmured, cradling her as they both

tried to balance on the divan, which didn't have quite enough room for them to lie side by side. "Unbelievable."

"Absolutely." Since they were starting to slide, Nora added, "How about moving into the bedroom?"

"Great idea."

In her queen-size bed, she curled against Leo's broad chest and wondered how long it would take before they could do this again. She definitely craved a repeat. Maybe a whole series of them, hour after hour. Because making love to Leo was a once-in-a-lifetime treat, for many reasons. *Younger than me, not ready to have kids, too handsome for my own good.*

Her mind stuck on the too-handsome part as she bathed in Leo's masculine scent. Oh, yes, he was well worth having again and again, before they went their separate ways tomorrow. All she needed was a short nap and she'd be ready for action.

The next thing Nora knew, she was waking up to pale morning sunshine, a champagne headache and, beside her, an empty dent in the pillow.

Chapter Three

From the kitchen, Leo heard Nora moving around in the bedroom wing. Since he'd awakened early by habit, he'd indulged in a prowl through her condo. Three, count 'em, three bedrooms—one serving as a home office—and two and a half baths. His house was at best two-thirds this size.

Paid for with her share from the divorce. Yesterday, he hadn't given the subject much thought, but everybody in Safe Harbor knew who Reese Kendall was: president and founder of Kendall Technologies, which manufactured medical devices. The guy regularly made headlines with his charitable donations and art acquisitions.

Leo had learned from his father the importance of identifying the local power players. Besides, any police officer who planned to rise through the ranks was wise to pay attention. All citizens might be equal, but some required more kid-glove handling than others. And Reese was one of those.

As for Nora, she obviously had a career and position of her own. A prestigious, high-paid position. *Too rich for your blood,* Leo mused as he started the coffee. But since he wasn't in this for the long term, what difference did it make?

He opened the fridge and contemplated the pros and cons of eating leftover salmon, sauced chicken, steamed vegetables and almond rice for breakfast. The pros won. He filled a plate.

While he waited for it to heat in the microwave, he suddenly realized what he'd forgotten last night.

Protection. Damn.

He always carried a packet of condoms, but he hadn't been thinking straight. Still, while Nora had been tipsy, she wasn't completely blotto. Surely, as a doctor, she'd put herself on the pill or used some other form of birth control.

No sense worrying about it. Still, Leo felt irked at his carelessness.

Then he saw her emerge from the hallway.

Morning light touched her emerald eyes. Golden hair fell around the shoulders of a short, satiny robe that gapped to reveal the curve of her breasts. His whole body came alive with longing.

The way he responded, you'd think he was starved for sex, Leo reflected. And the way she'd gone at him last night, he could almost swear she'd been starved for sex, too, but that seemed wildly unlikely. The single males who worked at the hospital would have to be dead below the waist to miss her unrepressed sensuality.

Thank goodness he and Nora were both consenting adults who knew the rules of engagement. When the fun ended, you walked away.

The timer rang. Leo ignored it. "You look great."

She blinked. "I'm glad you're still here. Mmm. Smells delicious."

He removed the plate and handed it over, as if he'd fixed it for her all along. "Coffee?"

"Yes, please." As she slid into a chair in the breakfast nook, the robe parted to reveal her long, slender legs. "My aspirin's starting to kick in, but I need caffeine."

Leo fixed another plate for himself and poured them both coffee. "Last night, we forgot something."

"Yes, we did." Nora paused with a fork halfway to her shapely mouth. "That would be D, E, F, G and H. I think we skipped all the way to Z."

"I've always wanted to try Q, R and S."

"Now?"

He reached over, removed the fork from her hand, and set it on the table. "What an excellent idea."

There was nothing underneath the robe, he discovered a moment later, and wished he hadn't bothered putting on his own clothes. Slacks, polo shirt—he didn't even finish getting out of them before he and Nora were on the carpet and he was forgetting about using a condom all over again.

SHE HAD TO BE OUT OF HER mind. Well, good, Nora mused, and forgot to think any further as she sailed through a series of climaxes and landed, breathing hard, on top of a thoroughly satisfied Leo. He *must* be satisfied, given all his groaning and gasping.

"Nice way to start the day," she murmured. "I'm sure glad it's Sunday."

"We could do this again nine or ten times," Leo observed.

"Don't you ever wear out?" Unwilling to move, she lay sprawled across him.

"I'm twenty-nine. I don't plan to wear out for years." Her cell phone rang. "Ignore it."

She wished she could. "I'm on call."

"That sucks."

"You said it."

Nora disentangled herself and retrieved the phone from her robe pocket. "Dr. Kendall." It took every ounce of concentration to sound cool and collected.

The nurse filled her in on the patient's condition. Labor progressing well, delivery less than two hours away. "I'll be there in an hour." As Nora clicked off, she remembered her car was at Tony's. "Can I ask a favor?"

A deep laugh rumbled from Leo. "Well, I'm not sure," he teased.

"I need to pick up my car, fast. I hate to hurry you, but babies don't wait." Nora sighed. "And I haven't even eaten breakfast."

He scrambled to his feet. "I'm an expert at eating and showering in a flash. It's practically an Olympic event for cops."

"I'll put my money on med students anytime."

"Go!"

Although it wasn't really a contest, Nora enjoyed the sense of friendly competition as she and Leo grabbed their plates and raced to the bathroom, snatching mouthfuls on the way. In the shower stall, she luxuriated in the pleasure of bumping against Leo, stealing kisses and tussling playfully for the soap.

She'd never felt this comfortable around Reese. He'd always seemed to be judging her. Positively, during the early years. That had changed gradually, Nora supposed. Then, in the months before his revelation about Persia, she'd caught him scrutinizing her with a touch of distaste.

She had to admit she'd gained ten pounds—fifteen on a bad day—since the wedding, but that was normal for a woman who'd reached her thirties. That shouldn't have been enough to alienate him. What had Reese expected, that his wife would stay in her twenties forever?

Leo was younger than her, she reflected as they toweled off. "You don't mind that I've got five years on you?" she asked, and watched for even a fleeting expression of dismay.

He grinned. "I like a woman with experience."

There was nothing glib or manipulative in his tone. Still, Nora assumed this sexy cop got plenty of practice in the bedroom. He probably had to chase women away with his baton. Of course he didn't mind the age difference, because their relationship was temporary.

Last night and this morning might have restored her sense of being desirable, but she'd be a fool to expect anything deeper. "You're a terrific guy. This was fun."

He paused, towel in hand, body splendidly naked. "Past tense? You make it sound as if it's over."

She shrugged apologetically. "Let's not kid ourselves. We both knew this was a one-time thing, right?"

He folded his arms, a movement that emphasized the muscles in his chest. "Why? Because I'm some eye candy you picked up at a wedding and now it's back to your real life?"

Where had that come from? Nora smacked him on the arm. "Get over yourself."

"Meaning what?"

"Meaning, I like you a lot, but a relationship? We aren't on the same page." She slipped into her lingerie.

"Because I'm a cop?"

He *was* touchy. "First of all, if I do get involved, I'd like there to be a strong possibility of children within the fore-seeable future." She stepped into a pair of slacks. "Second, you're a hunk and a half, and sooner or later you'll ditch me for some young hottie like my wife-in-law."

"Your what?"

"My ex-husband's new wife. The term kind of captures the love-hate relationship, don't you think? Except, in our case, it's mostly hate-hate." She fastened her blouse.

"I take it the breakup wasn't a mutual decision," he observed drily.

"A forty-two-year-old husband has an affair with his twenty-two-year-old executive trainee and declares that he's found his soul mate? No, it wasn't a mutual decision." Immediately, Nora regretted her sarcasm. "Sorry. I refuse to let anger poison my life. You've helped me get past a few of my issues, Leo. What I need next is a guy who's ready for the home-and-family thing, and I don't think that's you."

Strong hands framed her waist. As Leo's gray eyes fixed on hers, Nora nearly changed her mind. But a stopgap affair, no matter how appealing, could only weaken any chance she had of finding the right man in time to have a family.

"Damn shame," Leo muttered.

"Sure is." She could see in his expression that much as he'd like to argue, he agreed with her.

He released her, and they finished dressing. On the way out, he fetched a thermos from high in the cabinet and poured Nora a fresh cup of hot coffee to take to the hospital.

The guy truly was a keeper, she reflected with a twist of longing. For some other lucky woman.

A woman who had a few years to wait until Leo finished growing up.

By mid-March, the rains had nourished a profusion of spring flowers in the beds around the medical office building where Nora had a second-floor suite. She barely noticed the sunshine or the cheery pink and purple petunias this Friday afternoon, though, as she hurried along the sidewalk toward the hospital next door.

She'd spent so much time with her last patient that her nurse, Bailey Wayne, had pried her away by claiming there was an emergency call. While it was important to help her patient make an informed decision about treating menopause symptoms, Nora hated to be late for the first teleconference with the director of the hospital's planned new fertility program.

As if she weren't late enough, she had to pause to let a team of construction workers haul heavy equipment across the walkway and around the side. Work was under way in several parts of the hospital, including the installation of an embryology lab in the basement and the remodeling of offices on the fifth floor. Original plans had called for acquiring a nearby dental building to house the fertility center, but the purchase had fallen through at the last minute, and now everything had to be fitted here and there into existing structures.

She had barely started forward again when her cell rang. Without checking the readout, she answered, "Dr. Kendall."

"So you are still among the living." Leo's voice sent quivers through Nora.

Over the past three weeks, her dreams and daydreams had replayed their night together in a blur of longing and misgivings. Twice, he'd left messages, which she hadn't returned. Sticking to her guns and using her best judgment.

Then why did she feel overjoyed to hear from him? "I don't mean to be rude, but I thought I made my position clear."

"And I thought I made it clear I don't give up easily," he replied. "Don't tell me you couldn't use a stress buster."

Nora hurried through the staff entrance into the six-story medical center. "Is that supposed to sound romantic?" She flinched at the edge to her words. "I'm sorry. There's no reason why you *should* sound romantic."

"You're really not interested," he said ruefully. "Guess you didn't enjoy that night as much as I did."

Oh, yeah? Making love with Leo had banished a lot of the loneliness and rejection of the past year. Talking with him now aroused an almost painful craving to take refuge in his arms. How easily she could get involved all over again, if she let herself act like a fool.

Reaching the bank of elevators, Nora pressed the up button. "I'm late for a meeting. Leo, I'm glad you called but…"

"You aren't into me," he returned sharply. "I get it."

She hated antagonizing him. "This is for the best."

"I figured we'd both enjoy letting off a little steam. But it's no big deal."

"Thanks for understanding."

"Yeah. Have a nice life." He clicked off.

The elevator arrived. Riding alone, Nora wished she didn't have to worry about time and fertility, so she could afford to enjoy herself with Leo. She'd never felt so sexually compatible with a man before.

Since she'd matured physically as a teenager, people often took her for the cheerleader-sorority-girl stereotype, but she'd never been comfortable with relationships. If her mother hadn't died in a car accident when she was five, perhaps Nora would have developed better social skills during adolescence. At least she'd have had someone to ask about how to handle boys' demands and expectations.

Her father, a biology professor at the University of California, Santa Barbara, had encouraged Nora's studies, but he was clueless about her emotional side. And she'd been too shy to confide in her aunt, her father's sister, who lived a couple of hours away. Instead, she'd dealt with the awkwardness by burying herself in her schoolwork.

During college and med school, she'd had a few brief affairs, but nothing serious. Then she'd moved to Safe Harbor to take a staff position and had met Reese at a medical conference. Sophisticated and charming, he'd slipped past her defenses and won her trust.

Which showed how gullible she'd been.

The elevator stopped at the fourth floor, jolting Nora's thoughts back to the upcoming teleconference. This would be her first chance to find out what the world-famous, abrasive Dr. Owen Tartikoff had in mind. Although he couldn't leave his position in Boston for several months, he was already rumored to be planning policies that would change the way ob-gyns like her practiced medicine at Safe Harbor.

Outside the small auditorium, someone had set up a coffee urn and disposable cups. The way Nora's stomach was churning, she couldn't handle coffee, so she settled for a cup of tea instead.

Bracing for whatever revelations lay ahead, she shouldered open the door and slipped inside.

Chapter Four

"You don't need some snotty society babe anyway," Patty said as Leo slid into the patrol car and handed her a cup of black coffee from the corner café. No soy mocha latte crap for his partner.

"What do you mean?" He hadn't mentioned anything about calling Nora.

"You've got Whipped Puppy written all over your face." She put the car in gear and headed east along Ocean View Avenue, which had no ocean view and wasn't much of an avenue, either. "Take it from me, you'd just end up shooting clay pigeons."

When her high school boyfriend's rich parents broke them up, Patty had vented her wrath by demolishing clay pigeons on a firing range. She'd pictured each pigeon as the guy's head.

"She isn't snotty *or* rich," Leo protested. "She's a doctor."

"Yeah, they're a humble bunch."

Normally, he'd have agreed with the irony in his partner's comment, but something about Nora appealed to him. She was an odd mix of sophistication, intellect and ditsy blonde. Weird and hard to resist, or she would be if she hadn't just handed him his walking papers.

Then Patty said something that drove Nora completely from his mind. "I wonder what Captain Reed wants." They'd been ordered to return early from their shift and report to the detective captain's office.

"Whatever the brass dreams up, it's never good."

"Something to do with making detective," she surmised.

"Obviously." Leo, Patty and a bootlicker named Trent Horner were the three top scorers on the written promotional exam. They all had excellent performance evaluations and recommendations, and had expected to be scheduled for individual interviews. Instead, they'd received this puzzling instruction at briefing today.

"Don't take your bad temper out on me." Patty sniffed.

"Sorry."

"And don't apologize. Makes you sound like a wimp."

He grinned. "Yeah? Well, you can shove your thin skin where the sun never shines."

"That's more like it!"

Through the window, Leo noted a couple of teenage boys performing skateboard tricks over the curb. Not very safe, but they *were* wearing helmets and had the sense not to explode into the street in front of the cruiser. He decided to give them a break.

Besides, he didn't want to be the last to arrive. Trent was the kind of guy who'd turn any little thing to his advantage.

Patty made a couple of quick turns, eased past city hall and swung into the police-station parking lot. "Home, sweet home."

The two-story stucco building *had* become a home of sorts. After earning a master's degree in criminal science from Cal State University in nearby Long Beach, Leo had applied to a dozen police departments and received three offers. When it came time to decide between giant Los Angeles, a medium-size suburban community to the north and small Safe Harbor, he'd been surprised by the rush of affection he felt for his hometown.

His parents were both dead, and he'd been semi-estranged from Tony and his first wife, who gave Leo the impression she barely considered him worthy of her acquaintance. Although he'd had no personal reason to return here, as he'd weighed his options he'd discovered that he truly cared about this community and its people.

So he'd said yes. Now here he was, five years later, trying to prove he deserved to move up.

He and Patty emerged at the top of the rear staircase to find Trent already waiting in the detective bureau. The blond officer looked as if he'd stopped by the dry cleaner's to pick up his neatly pressed uniform and arranged for a professional cut and shave.

Through the window of a private office, Leo could see Captain Alan Reed talking intently with Sergeant Ed Hough. About what?

As they waited, Leo surveyed the open room, where he hoped to be working soon. On a Friday afternoon, most of the detectives were out in the field. Over in Juveniles, the desks were nearly clear of case files, in contrast to the vice/narcotics section, where the guys appeared to be composting heaps of papers, cups and takeout cartons, along with a copy of a girlie magazine that they probably claimed was research.

In the crimes-against-persons section, Mike Aaron sat tapping away at his computer. It was his position that would open up in a month. He and an old friend were buying a private detective agency.

The door to the captain's office swung open. Reed, his craggy face topped by gray hair, surveyed the three candidates coolly. "Come on in."

Trent reached the door first but waited to let Patty go

through. He should have known she hated gestures like that. Leo suppressed a grin as she trod on the guy's shiny leather shoe.

The three of them joined Reed and Hough around a small conference table. Despite the closed door, they were in full view of the bureau. Leo, who hated being on show, sat to one side with his face averted from the window.

The captain didn't bother with chitchat. "The chief has asked me to recommend one of you. You're all strong candidates, and neither Ed nor I feel ready to choose."

The sergeant, who'd been promoted to his position a mere six months earlier, was a meticulous investigator and a class-A paper-shuffler. A decent enough fellow, in Leo's estimation, but not the kind of person who inspired men and women to follow him.

"I'm reluctant to impose on Lieutenant Sellers," the captain went on. "He knows you better than we do, but he has other things on his mind right now."

"How's his daughter doing?" Patty asked.

"She's out of the coma, but there's a long road ahead." The thirteen-year-old had barely survived a car crash that killed the drunk driver who'd smashed into her father's vehicle. Sellers, a widower, had taken extended leave to care for his daughter.

"How can we prove our worth to you, sir?" Trent asked.

Leo suppressed a sarcastic crack. Did the guy have to be so oily?

"Ed and I agree that the best course is to observe the three of you closely over the next two weeks. We'll be looking for initiative, thoroughness and commitment. I can't be more specific than that. You all have strengths, so we'll be looking for qualities that make you stand out." The captain glanced at the sergeant. "Anything you care to add?"

Hough cleared his throat. "This isn't a contest pitting you against each other. I'd hate to see this degenerate into a squabble."

"Anyone undercutting their fellow candidates will be disqualified and reprimanded," the captain added. "Questions?"

"Is it all right if we put in extra hours?" Trent asked.

Touchy issue. "I can't authorize overtime," the captain said. "But we are willing to be flexible and allow a certain amount of leeway with your shifts on a case-by-case basis if you choose to undertake some special project."

Leo interpreted Patty's frown as confusion. She excelled at dealing with crises, especially calming potential confrontations where tempers ran high, such as domestic disputes. But strategic planning wasn't her forte.

As for Trent, no doubt he was already calculating how to position himself for maximum attention from the brass. Well, let him. Leo intended to go about this in a professional manner.

Since there were no questions, the captain dismissed the candidates. Hough followed them out and Trent, running true to form, asked to speak to the sergeant privately.

"What do you suppose he's up to?" Patty grumbled after the pair went off together.

"I refuse to worry about it."

"How about you?" she asked. "What's your plan?"

No sense trying to hide it. "I'm going to ask if I can shadow Mike."

Her face lit up. "That's a great idea. Let's both go."

"Hold on." The last thing Leo wanted was to put a wedge between him and his partner. Still, this was *his* idea. "Since I came up with this, why don't you pick someone else?"

"Because everybody else is out."

"They'll be back soon."

"Oh, come on." To Leo's dismay, Patty wheeled and marched straight for Mike's desk. It had never occurred to him that his pal would commandeer his idea.

Of course, she didn't see it that way, he realized as he heard her announce, "Hey, Mike, how about Leo and I shadow you? You can show us the ropes and we'll take some of the load off you."

The detective dragged his gaze from the computer screen. "Both of you? Leo can find his own mentor."

"Well…" Patty wavered. "It was his idea."

"You beat him to it," Mike pointed out. "Besides, you're prettier than he is." The detective's easy manner belied the flirtatious words. Although single, he'd never treated Patty as anything other than one of the guys.

Leo gritted his teeth. Whatever he said now would sound like sour grapes.

Patty shot him an apologetic look. "Sorry, Leo."

"Don't apologize. It makes you sound like a wimp."

Hearing her own words brought a rueful nod. "I guess what's done is done."

"So what're your plans for tomorrow?" Mike asked her.

They were scheduled to patrol. But the captain had offered to be flexible, so Leo shrugged and left Patty to make arrangements.

Across the room, Trent and Hough emerged from the sergeant's office and shook hands. The bootlicker had his course under control, obviously.

Leo supposed he could find another detective to shadow, but there was no one he respected as much as Mike. Besides, the captain had mentioned showing initiative and standing out. Imitating his two rivals wouldn't accomplish either of those goals.

Usually, in a situation like this, he talked things over

with Patty. Not this time, he decided as he skimmed down the stairs to the locker room. Second choice for a sounding board might be Tony, but while Leo sometimes asked his brother about legal issues, he preferred to forge his own path when it came to his career. Chalk it up to a lingering adolescent rivalry, but he wanted his victories to be strictly his own.

An image of Nora flashed onto his mental screen. Talking things over with her might help clarify his thoughts. But after the way she'd shot him down, that was out of the question.

He'd be handling this one alone. And he'd better come up with a plan fast.

"I CAN'T BELIEVE THAT man!" Sitting at a table in the hospital cafeteria, Nora downed another bite of her early dinner special, which tonight consisted of roast chicken, lemon rice and a vegetable medley. Usually, she ate salad for dinner, but today she felt ravenous. Being infuriated at Dr. Tartikoff apparently stimulated her appetite, which didn't bode well for her waistline in the coming months.

"It sounds like I missed quite an introduction to the great Dr. T.," Samantha Forrest observed over a cup of coffee. The pediatrician had caught Nora in the hallway after the teleconference and suggested they get together for a chat.

Neither woman had much time for socializing, and Nora appreciated the offer. She needed to unload on *someone*.

Sitting in the darkened auditorium, she'd listened in dismay as the renowned specialist, teleconferencing from his office in Massachusetts, had laid out his plans. He intended to put Safe Harbor Medical Center's new fertility program on the medical map, and never mind who got run over on the way.

"He didn't cite me by name, but he singled out some of

my cases as bad examples." While Nora disliked having
the new fertility director go through her patient records,
technically the patients' right to confidentiality didn't bar
a medical superior from reviewing treatment plans. "It appears I don't take enough of a high-tech approach to suit
him."

"Mark mentioned something about him wanting to
achieve the highest pregnancy rate in California." Although
her pediatric practice wasn't directly linked to the new program, Sam clearly kept tabs through her husband.

Stab, stab went Nora's fork. She sent her target, a lima
bean, scurrying over the edge of the plate, where it hid
from sight. "He said *one doctor*—that would be me—had
a patient undergoing traditional hormone treatments for
three years until she gave up and decided to adopt. I guess
he didn't read the part about her religious objections to *in
vitro*."

"He does have a reputation for being bullheaded."

"And I can't believe he..." Hearing the ring of her own
voice, Nora glanced around. Nobody occupied the tables
close by, but she lowered the volume all the same. "He
mentioned that this same doctor has another couple who're
taking it slow when they might already have achieved pregnancies. Sure, by bankrupting themselves!"

The couple in question were in their late twenties and
lacked insurance coverage for infertility. Since their youth
allowed them a few years' latitude, they'd chosen to try
less-expensive procedures first.

"You aren't directly under his supervision," Sam commented. "Not like his research fellows."

"He's supervising *all* the infertility cases here," Nora
reminded her. While those constituted only part of her practice, it was an important part. "He actually lectured us about
upgrading our skills, as if we don't already attend seminars

and keep current with research. The problem is, he sees this as strictly a technological issue. He doesn't seem to grasp that it's also about emotions, finances, the whole range of patients' lives."

"You don't have to persuade me. Besides, he can't order you to go against a patient's wishes," Sam reminded her. "And Mark will back you up."

"Yes, but I know the pressure he's under." Everyone was aware how badly the corporate owner, Medical Center Management, wanted to develop a lucrative, world-class fertility program.

"You're a great doctor—I'm on your side," the pediatrician declared.

Impulsively, Nora reached across and patted Sam's arm. "I appreciate that."

"I mean it."

"Thanks." Nora studied her empty plate, puzzled. Had she eaten everything?

"Speaking of what a great doctor you are," Sam went on, "we could use your help with the counseling center."

"Oh?" Nora braced for the latest request to lend her expertise to the sometimes shaky project Sam had launched last fall with little more than goodwill and enthusiasm. Its fancy name—the Edward Serra Memorial Clinic—couldn't disguise the lack of funding or the fact that the program, based at the city's community center, depended on volunteer staff and peer counselors.

Nora applauded the goal of providing information and a sympathetic ear to teen parents, abused women and families in crisis, but there were other, better funded and better organized programs to help them. That was why she'd resisted Sam's urging to get involved.

"I know we're rough around the edges, but nobody else does what we do." The pediatrician leaned forward, blue eyes ablaze. "Many of our clients mistrust red tape and snoopy bureaucracies. They like being able to wander in without an appointment and just talk to somebody."

"Which does *not* have to be an obstetrician," Nora pointed out. "I already work at a free clinic several times a month, and my nurse volunteers for you. Why don't you ask Bailey to see them?"

Sam ignored the question. "There are a couple of girls I'm concerned about. You'd be perfect to counsel them."

"Do they have medical issues?" Nora was willing to offer advice in her field of expertise.

"Not specifically, but they have problems related to their pregnancies. Like, what to do with the babies." Quickly, her friend pushed onward. "They both tend to drop by on Saturday afternoons. Guess it's hard to roll out of bed early when you're pregnant."

"It's hard to roll out of bed early, period." Recently, Nora had started setting two alarm clocks, one placed halfway across the bedroom to make sure she didn't dive back under the covers and fall asleep.

"Come in tomorrow afternoon and say hello. Pretty please. Their names are Violet and Suzy. You've got the perfect opening—just ask if they have any medical questions. They do get prenatal care through the county, but they're pretty hit-or-miss about keeping their appointments."

Nora had to admire her tenacity. "All right. I'll assess the situation. Once."

"Fabulous! I've been hoping we could add an obstetrician to our roster. Now, if we could find a few guys to counsel the teen dads, we'd be set. I was hoping Mark would find time, but he prefers to play with the triplets, and I can't blame him." Mark and Samantha were adopting three adorable infants.

"Don't add me to your roster. I'm stopping by only once."

Nora gave her plate another baleful look, affronted by its emptiness.

"I'll let Eleanor know you're coming." Eleanor Wycliff, a volunteer from Los Angeles, coordinated the counseling center.

Nora had been looking forward to sleeping late on Saturday and then hanging around the house in her bathrobe. Too late to back out, though. "Okay."

After her friend departed, Nora stood near the serving line, debating the nutritional merits of rice pudding for dessert. She didn't usually like bland food, but after suffering indigestion all week...

Chalky stomach. Increased appetite. Deeper sleep. Aversion to coffee. The symptoms added up.

Oh, please, no. Taking out her phone, Nora opened the organizer and checked the calendar.

Period. Late.

Which didn't necessarily mean anything, since she was often irregular, Nora told herself sternly. That was one of the reasons she'd been concerned about waiting too long to conceive.

But maybe she didn't need to worry about that anymore.

Much as she longed for a child, she hadn't wanted to get pregnant this way. Not unexpectedly. Not when she was under so much pressure at work. Above all, not by a man who had no interest in fatherhood.

Nora hurried to the building next door and let herself into her empty office. From habit, she checked her computer and noted the emails from patients and reminders from her nurse. She'd return the calls tonight.

First, she had a pregnancy test to take.

Chapter Five

For Leo, the Saturday shift started with a hardware-store burglary discovered by the owner when he arrived that morning. The alarm hadn't sounded and there were no obvious signs of a break-in, which pointed to an inside job. The storeowner admitted he hadn't changed the alarm code in years and suggested a recently fired worker as the suspect.

Leo documented everything for his report even more meticulously than usual. That was the best plan he'd been able to come up with—simply do his job exceptionally well and demonstrate as much initiative as possible.

"Too bad we have to hand this over to Crimes Against Property," Patty said as they sauntered out. "I bet we could wrap this up pretty fast. I mean, it's obvious who did this."

"Is it?" Leo returned. "Could be a current employee smart enough to know someone else would get the blame. Or an ex-wife with a grudge."

"You watch too many TV shows," his partner said.

"Yeah, probably."

The rest of the morning passed with routine traffic stops, a complaint about kids weaving their bikes through traffic—no sign of them on arrival—and a call about a loud argument at the beach. That turned out to be two actresses rehearsing a scene while working on their tans.

At noon, Leo dropped Patty off at the station house. She'd received permission to spend the last few hours of their shift with Mike.

"I'm sorry I stole your idea about shadowing him." She pushed back a strand of stick-straight hair. "And don't accuse me of sounding like a wimp. I mean it."

"You didn't do it on purpose." While not entirely placated, Leo saw no sense arguing over a done deal.

Besides, he didn't want to vent his ill temper on his partner. He'd awakened this morning grumpy, partly from drinking too much at a bar with some police buddies last night and partly because he'd been having sexy dreams about Nora.

Why did she have to wreck a good time? They were a perfect fit, and they'd barely gotten started. Usually women waited until the glow had faded before they brought up the old ball-and-chain business.

Yeah, he and Nora were a perfect fit, all right—in the bedroom. Outside of it, they moved in different worlds. Maybe if he were a corporate lawyer or owned a software company, she'd figure he was worth a little more of her time.

Half an hour before his shift ended, Leo cruised along the interconnected parking lots behind a group of civic buildings. The library looked busy, but nothing was amiss. He passed the fire department, where the guys were cleaning their equipment and probably figuring out what to fix for dinner, since they worked 24-hour shifts.

Behind the community center, which also housed the seniors' center and the Edward Serra Memorial Clinic, Leo saw only a half-dozen cars. Slow for a Saturday.

Normally, he'd have patrolled a few nearby streets and then headed back to complete his paperwork. But today,

rather than drive along enjoying the ride and the sea breeze
through the open window, he decided to check out the community center on foot. With so few people around and a lot
of expensive equipment sitting in those buildings, it was a
natural target for thieves. The sight of a uniformed officer
making the rounds ought to discourage such thoughts. And
he *had* vowed to show initiative.

The back door of the community center pushed open with
barely a creak. To his right, through a glass door marked
Office, he saw an older woman working at a computer.
Toward the front, in the larger of two meeting rooms, a
couple of men were setting up tables for what, according
to a flier on the bulletin board, was a local charity's annual
awards dinner taking place tonight.

Nothing wrong here. That was a good thing, Leo reminded himself.

Outside, he strolled around to the annex, which a couple
of now-defunct local clubs had used for headquarters over
the years. Then the Serra clinic, founded at the hospital,
had gotten kicked out to make room for the new fertility
center. Leo had heard about that from his brother and Kate,
who'd volunteered as a peer counselor until baby Tara came
along.

The entrance to the annex lay on an alley. The door stood
wide-open, which Leo supposed made sense for a drop-in
counseling clinic, but you never knew who else might come
by. He doubted the staff inside the main building would
notice if there were trouble here.

As he approached, a girl's angry words drifted out the
doorway. "How many times do I have to tell you I'm not
interested? Leave me alone!"

Might be a heated discussion. But domestic disputes
could turn violent.

Approaching cautiously, Leo peered into the sparsely

furnished front room. The only person in sight was a young man facing in the opposite direction. All Leo could see was slick dark hair, baggy pants and an oversize T-shirt. Despite the garb, there was no obvious gang insignia or tattoos.

"It's my baby, too." The young man addressed someone in a second room, out of view.

"Oh? You planning to raise it by yourself?" the girl demanded in the same strident tones as earlier.

"Suzy, I want to marry you. What's wrong with that?" the fellow pleaded. "I can take care of you."

Leo relaxed marginally. So far, this guy's manner appeared peaceable enough.

"Yeah, you've told me that like a million times!" the girl screeched. "What does it take to get it through your thick head? I'm not giving up college for you or anybody else. I'm entitled to my dreams."

"What about my dreams?" the boy demanded.

"Leave me out of them!"

"What about our baby?"

"As long as it's in *my* body, it's *my* business."

From the inner room, a woman said, "Ralph, let's make an appointment so you and I can talk privately."

Her velvety voice shimmered through Leo. He'd had no idea Nora was volunteering here. What idiot had left her alone to handle such a volatile situation?

"So you can tell me I'm wrong and she's right?" the youth snapped.

Time to make his presence known. Keeping back to avoid invading the boy's personal space and perhaps arousing a fight-or-flight reaction, Leo said, "Everything okay here?"

Ralph whirled, his fists clenched. No tattoos on his broad, high-boned face and no indications of a weapon,

Leo observed. Also, when the boy saw the uniform, his anger visibly deflated. Respect for authority—good.

A chair scraped and Nora appeared. With her long hair tucked behind her ears and wearing a loose sweater and jeans, she could have passed for a college student. "Leo!" She sounded relieved.

"Everything okay?" he repeated.

"We were just talking."

She moved aside, making way for a Hispanic teenager, whose eyes lit up when she spotted his uniform. "Officer, this guy is harassing me."

Ralph stared at her. "I was not!"

"He won't leave me alone." She twisted a strand of dark hair around her finger. With only a slight thickening of the waist, the girl didn't appear very far along in her pregnancy.

Leo had to respect her claim, even if it seemed exaggerated. "I'll be happy to take a report. If you need me to issue a temporary restraining order…"

"I'm not stalking you, Suzy! Are you trying to get me arrested? I'll lose my job." Ralph stared disbelievingly at the girl. "I'm trying to be a good guy. I don't want to run out on my family like my dad did."

"I'm not your family." Suzy pressed her lips together.

Nora glanced at Leo uncertainly. She might be an expert in her field, but obviously no one had trained her to deal with this kind of incident.

If Patty were here, Leo would separate the couple and talk to the boy privately while she interviewed the girl. Working alone, he had to make sure Suzy's rights were protected. On the other hand, he hated to see a young man slapped with a restraining order that might affect his employment.

He took out his pad. "I'll need to see some identification

from both of you." Might as well let them know this was serious business.

Suzy's eyes widened. "I didn't mean it. He isn't stalking me."

"Are you sure?"

The girl nodded. "I'm just not interested in getting married and keeping the baby, and I wish he'd quit harping on it."

"We can work this out." Ralph gave Leo a sideways glance. "I mean, that's my opinion."

"Suzy and I need to finish our counseling session," Nora said. "Ralph, I'll be happy to meet with you next Saturday if you'll come by around one."

Now that tempers had calmed, Nora was taking charge. Leo admired her quiet resolve.

"It won't do any good," Ralph grumbled.

"Why don't you cool down and then give the clinic a call?" Leo told him.

"I guess you think I'm some kind of criminal," the boy muttered.

"Actually, I think you're a responsible guy who cares about your girlfriend," Leo answered honestly. "Most men would hang on to their freedom. Have you thought about what it's going to mean to raise a kid? There'll be medical bills and temper tantrums, and before you know it, you'll have a teenager who tells you where to get off."

"I don't want to be like my dad," the boy said stubbornly. "He dumped us when I was five."

That meant the kid had no father to talk to, Leo mused. While his own father had been physically present, they'd never discussed anything that mattered. Leo had missed that. "If you need somebody to unload on, maybe I can help."

"You mean, like a counselor?" Ralph asked.

Leo hadn't intended that, exactly. But catching the glimmer of appreciation in Nora's eyes, he decided it wasn't a bad idea. "Sure. I get off duty in a few minutes. My name's Leo Franco, by the way."

"I'm Ralph Trueblood. But I have to work. At the supermarket," the boy added. "I could come by next Saturday, like the lady said."

Leo had that day off. "Fine. I'll see you here at one."

They shook hands. As Ralph departed, it hit Leo that he'd volunteered for something that had no bearing on his quest to make detective. He ought to be spending his free time on more productive pursuits.

No matter how annoyed he'd felt about Nora's rejection, he was still a sucker for her. Seeing her gorgeous mouth stretch into a smile, Leo didn't regret what he'd done. Not one bit.

Nora hadn't expected the volunteer director to leave early and put her in charge. Then, while she and Suzy were reviewing how to relinquish a baby for adoption, Ralph had showed up.

Although the boy didn't act threatening and she sympathized with his position, Nora understood how touchy a situation like this could get. Leo's arrival felt like a reprieve.

Also, he looked great in a uniform. The blue shirt set off his brown hair, and despite the heavy cluster of equipment around his hips, it was obvious he kept his body in great shape. Well, she knew that already, didn't she?

Then she remembered that she needed to talk to him about an issue he was not going to like. Well, maybe some other time, when she'd had a chance to prepare what she wanted to say.

"I can stick around till you're done," Leo told her and Suzy. The concern in his eyes nearly made Nora forget how fast it was likely to change into—what? Resentment? Denial? "This place is kind of isolated."

"Oh, we're not alone." Nora gestured toward the small office next to the counseling room. "There's a computer guy upgrading our system."

Leo frowned and glanced inside. "I should have noticed someone else was here."

"The way Ralph was carrying on?" Suzy said, as if she hadn't contributed her share of noise.

Leo shook his head, clearly annoyed with himself. "I don't usually make mistakes like that."

"I guess you were distracted." And so was Nora. So distracted she only now noticed a new face peering in the front door, a young girl with Vietnamese features and a bulging abdomen that indicated she was well into her third trimester. "You must be Violet Nguyen. Dr. Sam said you might stop by. I'm Nora Kendall."

The arrival of the second girl provided an even better excuse to postpone talking to Leo. Still, putting off their discussion wasn't going to make it any easier.

The girl edged inside, her wary gaze fixing on Leo's uniform. "What's going on?"

"Routine patrol." He checked his watch. "Got some reports to write. Well, since you have company, I'll be on my way. Don't stay here alone."

"I won't." Nora enjoyed the sight of his powerful body striding away. "Violet, if you'll let Suzy and me finish up, I'll be with you in a couple of minutes."

"Oh, I'm done." Suzy fetched her purse and gave Nora a hug. "You were great, Dr. Kendall."

"I'm not sure I told you anything you couldn't have found on the internet," she admitted.

"It feels different, hearing it from a doctor. I'll see you next Saturday." With a wave, the girl went out.

Next Saturday? Nora hadn't committed to counseling more than once. Still, she ought to see Suzy through another session or two. They'd established a connection, and it would be a shame to break it now. Although the girl seemed determined to give up her baby, she might have second thoughts as the pregnancy progressed.

"Come on inside." Nora had looked up Violet's file in advance, but found only sketchy information. No home address, only a cell-phone number, and no medical or other records. Nothing to confirm her age, either, which was listed as eighteen. Given her shy manner, she might be younger.

Eleanor, the director, had made it clear the clinic didn't pressure its clients for ID. To do that might chase away the very people they wanted to help.

"You're a doctor?" The girl followed Nora into the counseling room, which featured a worn love seat, a couple of chairs and a low, child-size table with crayons and pads of paper.

"Yes. Do you have any medical questions?" Nora estimated Violet to be about seven months along.

A head shake sent the girl's straight hair swinging.

"What would you like to talk about?"

"My boyfriend won't give me money," she said. "My mom's mad at me and… Is it wrong to keep my baby?"

Nora felt a rush of empathy. She understood the overwhelming love and longing for a child, and now that she carried one inside her, she couldn't imagine relinquishing it to someone else.

If Violet wanted to raise her child, she faced a long and difficult road. But the obstacles weren't insurmountable. "It isn't wrong at all. You're already receiving medical care, I understand. Has anyone arranged for you to talk to a social worker?"

"No social worker!" Pushing back her chair, the girl rose heavily to her feet.

"Only to help you apply for state aid." Nora tried to decide how to proceed. With her regular patients, she offered advice and then sat back while they reached their decisions. By contrast, Violet was barely an adult—and that was assuming she hadn't lied about her age. "There are several programs you should qualify for, but we have to get started on the paperwork. These things take time."

Violet opened the door. "My boyfriend comes from a rich family. They should help me."

"You said he refused," Nora pointed out.

"I'll make him change his mind."

The boy did have legal obligations. "Let's talk about finding you a lawyer."

"I have to go." Clearly, the discussion made Violet uneasy.

"You'll come back next Saturday?" Although Nora wanted the girl to stay today, she couldn't force her. "I'll research legal aid."

"Maybe." Swiveling away, Violet gave a start at the sight of a stocky young man flipping through a magazine in the lobby. "Oh! I didn't know anyone was here."

"I'm Ted Chong." He pushed his glasses higher on his flat nose. "I was waiting to tell Dr. Kendall I've updated the programs."

"I'm Violet." The girl shook hands politely.

Although these two, with their Asian backgrounds, might appear to be from the same culture, Nora knew that the main culture they shared was American. Orange County was reputed to have the largest Vietnamese population in the world outside of Vietnam itself. Many of the families, possibly including Violet's, had arrived as refugees since the fall of Saigon. By contrast, Ted's family was Chinese, and most Chinese immigrants came here for economic and educational reasons. The cultures retained distinctly different native languages and traditions, even as the younger generations blended in with their Californian peers.

"Thanks, Ted." Nora had immediately liked the young man, whose mother, May Chong, worked as administrative secretary at the hospital. She also volunteered at the center.

"I can walk Violet to her car," he offered. "The pavement's kind of uneven. Don't want a pregnant lady to trip."

"That's kind of you," Nora said. "Violet?"

"Okay. Thanks." The girl let Ted take her elbow and help her across the parking lot.

What a contrast to Suzy and Ralph's situation, Nora reflected as she watched them go. Bringing in a lawyer and dragging Violet's boyfriend through court might produce some money, but reluctant fathers often caused so much stress and wasted time that in the end the mom earned every cent she received.

Speaking of reluctant fathers, Leo's remarks to Ralph hadn't been reassuring, she mused. The man clearly had negative expectations of parenthood.

It had been such a pleasure to see Leo that she wished she didn't have to break the news about her pregnancy. How was she going to approach him? Waiting until next Saturday didn't seem fair, but she could hardly barge into the police station like some heroine in a melodrama and declare that the handsome officer had done her wrong.

Actually, he hadn't done her wrong. Or, if he had, she wished he'd do the same wrong again a few dozen times before she had to enlighten him about the consequences.

Great, Nora. You're being totally mature about this. Besides, she'd already resigned herself to giving him up, hadn't she?

As Eleanor had instructed, Nora shut down the computer, turned off the lights and locked the door. The annex lacked an alarm system, which reminded her of Leo's concerns about safety. For the most part, Safe Harbor lived up to its name, so she wasn't too worried about interlopers, but angry boyfriends and ex-husbands of clients were another matter.

Nora appreciated the sight of Ted lingering outside. Beyond him, the parking lot looked almost empty. "Did she get off okay?"

He fell into step beside Nora as she headed for the main building to leave the key. "Yeah, but there's a lot of stuff piled in her car. I hope she isn't sleeping in it."

That possibility hadn't occurred to Nora. "She refused to let me contact a social worker." Another concern struck her. "I'm not even sure she's of age. You don't suppose she's a runaway, do you?"

From his pocket, Ted extracted a slip of paper. "I wrote down her license-plate number. Figured you might be able to get an address and check on her."

"You're terrific. You're wonderful to help out at the center this way." Gratefully, Nora accepted the paper.

"Hey, it's fun. See you around." He sauntered away.

After dropping off the key, Nora sat in her car, studying the plate number and wondering if Leo was still at the police station directly across Civic Center Drive. This was the perfect excuse to stop by.

Her stomach churned, and she dug a small packet of crackers out of her purse. At the moment, she couldn't tell the difference between morning sickness and nerves. Did she *have* to tell Leo today?

Quit dawdling. She should get this over with.

Nora didn't kid herself that Leo was going to get on one knee and offer marriage. He wouldn't dance a jig around the police department, either. But talking to him there might at least keep both their tempers on an even keel.

She didn't need his money, and these days a single mom's reputation wouldn't suffer. In fact, she'd be willing to let him off the hook entirely, as long as he signed away his paternal rights. But what a shame for her baby not to know his or her father. And what a shame for a loving uncle like Leo to miss out on being part of his own child's life.

Nora had no idea how she was going to broach the subject. She'd simply have to play it by ear. At the same time, she also had to make sure Violet wasn't a scared kid living in her car.

Chapter Six

Filling out paperwork was the least fun part of this job, Leo thought as he transferred his notes about the hardware-store burglary into the computer. Every crime had to be documented in detail, both for the sake of the investigating officer and so it would stand up in court. In the hands of a wily defense attorney, any discrepancy or omission could be used to free a criminal.

Of course, proper recording also protected the falsely accused. Leo didn't see a lot of that, but he knew it happened. In theory, anyway.

Alone in the report room, he scarcely noticed the routine noises of the police station: the dispatchers answering calls and directing patrol cars; the watch commander and the desk sergeant discussing the Lakers' chances of making the NBA finals; someone cursing at a recalcitrant vending machine in the break room.

Nearby, the creak of leather shoes made him look up. Mike Aaron had come in, which seemed odd, since detectives had their own desks.

"That the hardware-store break-in?" He indicated Leo's screen.

Puzzled, Leo nodded. Crimes Against Persons handled murders, robberies, sex crimes and assaults. Since the victim hadn't been present during the burglary, this was a property crime, and therefore not Mike's territory. "What's on your mind?"

The detective folded his arms. His reserved manner had long ago earned Leo's respect, but he never hung out with the guy.

"You put Patty's idea in your write-up?" Mike asked.

"Excuse me?"

"That it might be a current employee setting up the guy who got fired?"

What the hell? "First of all, I don't speculate in my reports," he told Mike. "Second, that was my idea, which she dismissed. Third, when did this become your damn business?"

Mike's jaw worked. He'd overstepped; even he had to see that. "You have a point."

"Three points."

"If you say so." Mike's chin jutted out. "Patty's a smart girl, smarter than people give her credit for. Part of the reason is that she's always deferring to you. I don't like seeing her taken advantage of."

Leo had an uncomfortable idea where this was going. "You trying to date her?"

Mike's eyes narrowed. "Of course not."

"Well, if there's anyone underestimating Patty in this room, it's you," Leo fired back. "My partner doesn't need protecting. She's one tough cookie. So back off."

It wasn't the most diplomatic way to talk to a man who might influence the higher-ups. Still, Leo had no intention of letting some interfering or jealous or simply misguided colleague push him around.

"I'm just saying." Mike let the enigmatic remark hang in the air.

"Saying what?"

With a tight shake of the head, the detective turned away.

The guy was leaving in a month, and he'd never showed any particular interest in Patty's situation until now, as far as Leo knew. What was his agenda?

No sense getting into any further argument. But Leo didn't like the way this rivalry for promotion was shaping up. The last thing he wanted was to end up estranged from Patty, whether due to gossip or because Mike managed to persuade her Leo really *had* stolen her ideas.

Irritably, he pushed a key to send his report to the patrol sergeant. Near the door, he heard Mike scuff to a halt, and glanced up.

No question what had startled the detective. Stunning blonde, tight jeans, loose deep pink sweater that failed to disguise the swell of her breasts. Leo's body got hot, and he decided that if Mike went after Nora, he *would* call the guy the out.

"Hi. Can you tell me where to find…" Her green eyes widened as they met Leo's. "Oh, there you are."

"Hey." He hoped his grin didn't look as goofy as it felt.

She radiated a smile back at him that lit up the entire police station.

"Friend of yours?" Mike's eyebrow lifted. Although he could easily have passed Nora and exited, he didn't.

With introductions unavoidable, Leo went formal. "Detective Aaron, this is Dr. Kendall."

"There's no medical emergency, I hope?" Mike asked.

"Just a question regarding the counseling center." Nora stopped, clearly uncertain how freely to speak.

"I'd be glad to help," the detective said. "Leo's not much of an expert on counseling."

"He's better than you think," Nora replied.

Good one. Now beat it, Mike.

"Really?" The guy was *not* taking hints today.

"Really." Nora folded her arms, looking every inch the lofty physician. A very feminine lofty physician.

Mike swallowed hard. "If you're sure…"

"Yes, but thanks for the offer."

"Anytime." With a sigh of unmistakable regret, Mike finally got going.

"I didn't mean to interfere with anything," Nora said when they were alone.

"You aren't." Leo couldn't resist asking, "How'd you get back here? Usually the desk officer runs a tight ship." Visitors were supposed to remain in the lobby unless personally escorted.

"He was very friendly," Nora said.

I'll bet. "What can I do for you?" Leo pulled out a chair beside his station.

She glided into the seat. "That girl who arrived as you were leaving, Violet Nguyen. From the amount of stuff in her car, it looks like she might be living in it, and we don't have much information about her. She seems so young. I'm concerned she might be a runaway."

If that were the case, Nora had a legitimate concern. "I'll check for reports. You didn't happen to see her driver's license, did you?"

"Ted Chong, our computer guy, copied down her plate number." She handed him a slip of paper.

A quick check of the DMV database informed Leo that the car was registered to a Rose Nguyen of Safe Harbor. A little more probing turned up the information that the owner had a business license for a flower shop called Rose's Posies here in town. There was no report of a runaway daughter or missing car.

"Looks like she's driving Mom's wheels. Florists tend to cart around a lot of supplies, which might account for the clutter in the car." Reluctant to dismiss Nora's concern, he added, "If you have any reason to think the girl might be in danger..."

She shook her head, a movement that loosened a curtain of hair. Leo remembered all too well its silky texture between his fingers and how, spread across a pillow, it caught the morning light.

"Thanks for checking." Nora startled as footsteps passed in the hallway. "Busy place, huh?"

"Quite a change from the clinic. I don't like the idea of you working there alone. And don't tell me having a computer guy on the premises constitutes security."

She gave a light cough. "It was my first day counseling. I'll admit, Suzy's boyfriend caught me off guard. Thanks for offering to talk to him."

"Sure. Why not?" Leo was pleased that she showed no signs of hurrying away. Was it possible she'd changed her mind about yesterday's brush-off? Leo was now off duty, and he'd like nothing better than to spend a Saturday night with her.

Yeah, he could imagine what Patty would say about him being a pushover for sexy blondes. But Nora wasn't like other women he'd dated. He enjoyed just sitting and talking to her.

Among other things.

Leo jerked out of his reverie as Trent Horner, blond hair parted to reveal the pink of his scalp, poked his nose into the room. "I heard there was a problem at the counseling center."

Damn gossip. "Don't you have something useful to do, like help the sergeant shuffle papers?" Leo snapped.

"Liaising with the other departments is an important responsibility," Trent returned indignantly.

So that's what Hough had assigned him. True, coordinating investigations with traffic and patrol was an important management function. On the other hand, Leo doubted Trent was doing much more than glorified clerical work.

Or so he hoped. He'd feel better if he could come up with a strategy to distinguish himself from his competitors.

Meanwhile, Trent was busy introducing himself to Nora and making solicitous inquiries. "Thanks, but there's no problem at the counseling center that Leo can't handle," she said, to which Leo responded with a silent cheer.

Trent lingered. "You're a doctor? Or is that a Ph.D., like a psychologist?"

"She's an ob-gyn. Since you aren't married or involved, the only way you'd need her services is if you're contemplating a sex change. Are you?" Leo shot back.

Nora laughed, then clapped a hand over her mouth. Just when Leo was hoping Trent would catch on and let them have a private conversation, he spotted Captain Reed.

Usually, the higher-ups had better things to do on the weekend than hang around the station. But with the lieutenant on leave, Leo supposed the captain was putting in extra hours.

Reed gave Nora a friendly nod and introduced himself. "I couldn't help overhearing. Is something wrong at the counseling center?"

Nora shook the captain's hand. "It's a pleasure to meet you. Wow, I'm surprised there's so much interest in the center."

"Dr. Kendall and I were discussing the situation," Trent began.

"Didn't I hear the sergeant ask you to hurry up with something?" the captain said.

"Oh, uh. Yes, sir." And off, finally, he went.

Reed fixed his attention back on Nora. "It's not often a distinguished member of the medical community pays us a visit. What can we do to help?"

What a crock. He was flirting with her. Oh, great, Leo thought. Divorced and in his late forties, the captain was certainly eligible, but with one son in the army and another in college, he probably wasn't eager to become a dad again.

Not Nora's type. Of course, Leo reminded himself, neither was he.

"Officer Franco did us a big favor today," Nora was saying. "He noticed how secluded the facility is, so he came through on foot and defused a touchy situation with a client's boyfriend."

"Oh?" Reed raised an eyebrow, perhaps because there'd been no report of a disturbance.

"One look at the uniform and the guy backed down fast," Leo said.

"You came over here to thank him?" the captain asked Nora.

"Actually, I had a request," she replied. "He volunteered to come in next Saturday to counsel the young man, and I wanted to ask if he would also prepare some suggestions for us on security."

Was that why she'd lingered? Leo had hoped she had more personal matters in mind.

"I didn't realize he was qualified as a counselor." Beneath the captain's conversational tone, Leo felt him probing.

"The center uses peer counselors," Nora said. "Dr. Forrest usually gives them some training, but many of them already have experience working with patients. My nurse, Bailey, is one of our volunteers, for instance. And if a client has serious emotional issues, they're referred to a professional. Don't police officers learn conflict management and listening skills as part of their training?"

"Yes. However, I gathered Leo's partner was the one who mostly handled that area," the captain said.

"Well, judging by what I saw today, he's good at it, too."

Leo was surprised to learn Reed gave Patty all the credit for resolving conflict on the job. She *was* good at defusing situations, but he held up his end of things.

"I'll be counseling on my own time," Leo added.

Reed gave him an amused smile. "Glad to see you're willing to assist the good doctor." He shook Nora's hand again. "You're welcome at the station anytime."

"Thanks. I'll keep that in mind."

Okay, he was gone. Now, how was Leo going to persuade Nora to continue this discussion elsewhere?

He no longer bought the idea that she wasn't into him. Subtly but firmly, she'd risen to his defense in front of Mike, Trent and the captain. Leo didn't think her concern about Violet justified all that. In fact, she didn't have to come here today. She could have asked Dr. Forrest to pursue the question of whether the girl was a runaway.

Usually, he had no trouble making his case with a woman. *"I've got a couple of steaks we could barbecue...."* That should do the trick. Unless the sight of his less-than-fancy house put her off, but he no longer took Nora for a snob.

"Hey," Leo began.

"We should go somewhere private," Nora said.

He nearly choked. She'd beaten him to the punch. "Sure."

"You did say you were about to go off duty, right?"

"Yes, indeed."

"I'm parked outside. I could follow you home."

At the rate this was going, she'd walk in his front door and start stripping. Leo was definitely into that. "Sounds perfect."

She gave another small cough. Was that nerves? "I'm not

interfering with anything, am I? I mean, you probably had plans."

"Nothing I can't get out of." A couple of fellow patrolmen, Bill Sanchez and George Green, had mentioned a bring-your-own-beer-and-steak barbecue at their apartment complex. That hardly constituted a commitment.

"We need to talk. About…things."

"Always glad to talk about things," he said.

"Well, then." Did Nora have any idea what happened to that pink sweater when she took a deep breath?

"Give me a minute to change into street clothes." He decided against wearing his uniform home. Some women found the uniform a turn-on, but he didn't want to push his luck by suggesting she might enjoy removing it herself. Besides, he disliked wearing it off duty. Didn't want to set himself up as a target in case he ran into some troubled personality who had issues with authority figures.

"I'll wait right here."

Whoa—with an entourage of men, no doubt. "How about I meet you in the lobby?"

"Done," Nora said.

If there'd been a speed limit in the hallway leading to the locker room, Leo would have received a ticket. And gladly paid it.

Chapter Seven

Nora hadn't meant to give Leo the wrong idea. Judging from his reaction, he had high hopes for tonight. The problem was, she kept getting the wrong idea herself. Every time she looked at the guy, she wanted to rip off his shirt and run her hands over his hard chest.

She had to bring up the pregnancy, present him with the facts, but she wasn't eager to see his expression harden in response. Seriously, she didn't intend to make any demands. She was fine on her own.

Why did life have to be so complicated?

As her compact sedan followed Leo's red sports coupe along a series of side streets, she wished she were riding alongside him. That had felt good, practically sitting in his lap the night they drove to her condo. What had followed had felt even better….

Which was exactly how she got into this predicament.

Nora debated strategies. If she were Samantha Forrest, she'd walk into his house, face him and announce that she was pregnant.

Okay. She'd do it.

He lived on the east side of town, in a tidy neighborhood of small homes, many with charming touches such as rose arbors and striped awnings. No one would give Leo's house the Fairy Tale Cottage of the Month Award, though, Nora mused as she surveyed the boxy one-story dwelling fronted by a morose-looking evergreen hedge and a cracked cement porch. Near ground level, mud spattered the tan paint and the streaked white shutters cried out for a touchup.

Leaving his car in the driveway, Leo strode across a lawn patched with weeds. "I don't know why I put up with my gardener. Look at this lousy job."

"You don't have a gardener," Nora surmised after finding a parking space on the street.

"Sure, I do. It's me." He gave her a teasing grin that invited her to kiss it away.

"It's like putting up a sign that says Rebel Lives Here," she said.

Following her gaze, he studied the place as if seeing it afresh. "You think I'm acting out some kind of overgrown adolescent rebellion?"

"Tell me I'm wrong."

He seemed to be searching for a clever answer, and coming up dry. "I suppose I have to agree."

"My aunt says she can psychoanalyze people by their birdbaths," Nora remarked as they went up the walkway.

"I don't have a birdbath."

"I'm doing the same thing by psychoanalyzing your lawn," she explained. "Now surprise me with a decor out of *Better Homes and Gardens*."

"That would surprise me, too," Leo said as he let them inside.

A giant TV reigned over a living room studded with old couches and a scarred coffee table. Farther into the interior, worn carpeting gave way to scuffed linoleum in the kitchen and den. By contrast, the wood of the billiards table gleamed against the green felt surface.

Leo switched on a Coca-Cola stained-glass lamp. *"Mi casa es su casa."*

Officer Daddy

"Your casa is a little boy's fantasy," Nora replied, amused.

"I'd rather indulge in a big boy's fantasy." He watched her with what, to Nora, seemed like an intoxicating mixture of hope and desire.

She remembered her resolution to tell him about the pregnancy, but it went against the grain to hit him in the face with it. Besides, she was curious. "What's going on at the police station? I mean, maybe it's none of my business, but the captain acted like he was evaluating you."

"I'm up for promotion to detective," he said. "So's my patrol partner and that fellow who isn't having a sex change."

"No wonder the air was crackling." Thank goodness she'd followed her instincts and spoken on Leo's behalf. "I hope I didn't say anything wrong."

"Quite the opposite. I appreciated the testimonial." He moved to the table and lifted a triangular frame, freeing the bright-colored wooden balls. "You play pool?"

"Never tried it."

From a rack, he selected a middle-sized cue. "This looks about the right weight for you."

Did he have to keep changing the subject? Except, Nora recalled, she hadn't established a subject. "I'm not sure how to put this…"

Leo swiped the white tip across a blue cube sitting on the edge of the table. "The first thing you do is chalk your cue."

"You expect me to remember this?" she grumbled. "I'll probably never play pool again. In fact…"

"Right handed?" he asked.

"Yes, but…" The next thing Nora knew, she was holding the thick end of the cue stick in her right hand.

"Does that feel balanced?"

"Leo!"

"There any reason we can't talk and have fun at the same time?" His husky voice close to her ear sent tingles through Nora.

"You're good at this," she said wryly.

"Pool? You ain't seen nothin' yet." Standing behind her, he reached around to help aim her cue.

"I meant, seducing women."

A low chuckle caressed her nerve endings. "You ought to know." When she tensed, he added, "Do you realize pool originated as the French game of croquet? The nobles used to play it outside with wooden clubs, but they hated to sweat, so they moved it indoors. That's why the table's green. It's supposed to represent grass. Without weeds, you'll notice."

Nora started to laugh, but stifled it. She didn't mean to encourage him.

"Put your left foot forward and your right foot back." His hands moved to her hips. "Twist a little to the left so you won't block your own stroke. We wouldn't want to mess up a good stroke, would we?" From behind, his hardness brushed her derriere.

Heat flooded Nora. She shouldn't have suggested they come here. Should have insisted on neutral territory.

"Leo..." Fatal mistake, to swing around at that moment. His hands clasped her waist, his body pressed her lightly against the edge of the table and his mouth captured hers.

We need to talk.

Maybe later.

He smoothed up her sweater and explored her breasts with his tongue. It was astonishing how much she enjoyed unfastening his belt and stroking his chest, just as she'd longed to. Then he picked her up and, her legs wrapped around him, carried her into the bedroom.

Not the world's cleanest sheets. Nora didn't care. He forgot to use a condom, but that hardly mattered. It wasn't as if she could get pregnant again.

It felt wonderful having Leo inside her. Being free to kiss him, hold him, melt into him. By the time they both climaxed, she felt gloriously happy and like a complete idiot.

The happy part kept her quiet as Leo cradled her afterward. No sense spoiling this precious moment. Especially since it was unlikely ever to reoccur.

The doorbell buzzed.

"Forget it," he said.

They lay there, waiting for the person to go away.

Someone banged on the door so hard the sound reverberated through the house. Outside, a woman yelled, "Come on, Leo! I know you're in there. Your car's in the driveway."

"Oh, hell," he muttered.

Nora couldn't believe she'd landed in such a clichéd situation. "You have a girlfriend?" Couldn't be a wife; she'd have attended Tony and Kate's wedding. "You're cheating on her with me?"

Leo shot her a teasing look. "Jealous?"

What kind of response was that? "I'm annoyed." Nora threw off the sheets. "I took you for an honest man."

His grip on her wrist stopped her. "That isn't my girlfriend. It's my patrol partner, Patty."

She remembered what the captain had said. "She's the one who's good at conflict management?"

"So rumor has it."

"Present circumstances would indicate otherwise."

A sharp rapping shook the nearest window, making Nora jump. Thank goodness the blinds were closed. "Whatever you're doing, stop it! I need to talk to you," the woman called.

That makes two of us. For a horrifying moment, Nora wondered if Leo might have impregnated his patrol partner. But that hardly explained such urgency. A pregnancy could be discussed in due time. Nora winced at the irony of the thought.

"I'm coming, damn it!" Leo yelled.

Nora scrambled out of bed and went hunting for her clothes. She wondered if it might be possible to sneak out the front door while Patty was around the side, but no way could she retrieve her car without being noticed.

Besides, she hadn't done anything wrong. Stupid, maybe, but not wrong.

Tugging a T-shirt over his head, Leo passed her on his way out of the room. Nora barely got her shoes on before she heard the door open and a woman's strident voice say, "Mike told me he laid into you. You can't think I purposely stabbed you in the back."

"What else am I supposed to think?" Leo answered irritably.

"Why'd you take so long to answer the door? What were you doing, anyway?" The woman thumped inside.

Nora debated whether to pop out of the den and announce herself. The only alternative seemed to be hiding in a closet, so, cheeks burning, she sauntered into the front room.

"What do you think I was doing?" Leo replied at exactly the most embarrassing possible moment.

Patty's gaze raked Nora. "I should have guessed." Arrow-straight, straw-colored hair barely reached the patrolwoman's chin. Her stocky build made her seem large, although she stood only slightly taller than Nora's five foot seven inches.

"Patty, Nora. Nora, Patty." Leo dispensed with introductions in record time.

"You're the famous blonde." Patty was apparently referring to Nora's visit to the station.

"We're both blonde," Nora responded.

"She's observant," Patty told Leo. "Maybe you should get her to help you fill out your reports."

"I'd rather see her fill out a sweater," he answered crisply.

"Excuse me," Nora said. "That was rude."

Leo cast her an apologetic look. "You're right. Sorry."

"You stand up to him?" Patty asked. "Not bad. Oh, wait. You're that woman who used to be married to the rich guy."

"Leave him—her—out of this." Leo dragged his fingers through his hair, which sprang right up again. He turned to Nora. "Patty and I have issues to work out. I didn't mean for you to get caught in the middle."

Nora hated to go without telling him about the baby, but this hardly seemed like the right time. Besides, she'd be seeing him next Saturday.

Talk about issues. The guy had no clue.

"I was just leaving." Instinctively, she reached to tweak his cowlick into place, but it fell right back.

Patty's mouth quirked, as if the intimate gesture offended her. She didn't seem hurt or jealous, merely disgusted. But then, she'd obviously typecast Nora as an empty-headed socialite.

"It's Saturday night," Leo told Nora. "I was going to grill steaks."

"Something wrong with the barbecue at Bill and George's?" Patty fired the question at him. "Or aren't your old friends good enough for you anymore?"

Nora had no intention of sticking around and getting mired even deeper in their quarrel. "You guys can work this out. Rumor has it you're both really good at conflict resolution. See you later, Leo."

For a moment, she thought he might insist she stay, but she could see the anger seething beneath the surface, ready to discharge on his partner. Grabbing her purse, she made her getaway.

The baby could wait. What was one more week, anyway?

THE FACT THAT PATTY HAD driven Nora off made Leo even angrier. "Why did you take credit for my idea and then give Mike the impression I was trying to steal it from you?"

"I already apologized. Isn't that enough?" Her square jaw set pugnaciously.

"You didn't apologize."

"Did so."

"Is Mike trying to get into your pants or what?" He didn't exactly believe that, but it was a fair question.

"He's a friend. The kind you used to be," Patty snapped. "I've got as much right to get promoted as anyone."

"Who said you didn't?"

"You assume you're the most qualified, don't you?" She planted her hands on her hips.

"I *am* the most qualified." Seemed obvious to Leo. "Otherwise, why do you keep stealing from me?"

"Give one good example. No, wait, two." A pause. "Make that three."

"You mean, aside from shadowing Mike and fingering another employee in the burglary?"

"Yeah," she said. "Aside from those."

He couldn't help it. He started to chuckle. A minute later, Patty did, too.

"Do you concede the point?" Leo asked.

"I concede nothing." She shrugged. "I didn't mean to chase off your hot date."

"Yeah. That's a bummer." On the other hand, Leo did feel kind of constrained around Nora. He was keenly aware of how sensitive and smart she was. He hardly wanted her to see him tossing back beers and swapping off-color remarks with his buddies. "So, what were we supposed to bring to Bill and George's, anyway?"

"You mentioned steaks."

"Can't let those go to waste," he agreed.

As Leo stood on the porch and locked the door, he noticed how streaky the paint looked on the shutters. In fact, the entire front of the house had faded, and a crack in the porch appeared to be growing.

That was the trouble with dating a classy woman, he reflected as he followed Patty to her car as it was her turn to serve as designated driver. Being around Nora made him uncomfortably aware of the state of his house.

Next thing you knew, she'd turn him into his older brother. Much as he liked her, he refused to let that happen.

Chapter Eight

On Wednesday, Nora's stomach went into overdrive. For breakfast, she followed the advice she gave her patients— sip ginger ale and eat a slice of toast. By downing handfuls of crackers, she made it through the morning, but by lunch she could hold on no longer.

How many times had she placidly advised women that morning sickness was a normal sign of pregnancy and not a serious problem unless they encountered severe vomiting, dizziness or a racing heart? Never again would she gloss over the misery.

Struggling to keep control, Nora slipped out of her office and power-walked down the hall to the restroom. If she upchucked in her private office bathroom, her nurse would notice. In fact, it was surprising that Bailey hadn't remarked on her pallor already, but the nurse had been unusually pre-occupied this week. When Nora asked, she'd cited personal problems without elaborating.

Bracing herself in a restroom stall, Nora let nature take its course. What if this *was* a serious complication? she wondered. Some pregnant women developed a condition called hyperemesis gravidarum, a serious form of morning sickness that required hospitalization and treatment with intravenous fluids and medications.

Maybe she should see a doctor. Which brought up another

important point—who was she going to choose? For her regular checkups, she'd previously seen a woman gynecologist who'd recently moved out of state. There was no one she trusted more than Dr. Rayburn, whose office was conveniently located next to hers. They shared staff for records, billing and accounting. But he was her boss, and things might get awkward if she locked horns with Dr. Tartikoff.

As Nora straightened, she registered that the nausea seemed to be abating. In the absence of other symptoms, this was almost certainly normal, garden-variety morning sickness. No need to choose a doctor quite yet.

When she went to wash up, she discovered Dr. Rayburn's nurse, Lori Sellers, applying makeup at the mirror. "You all right, Dr. Kendall?" she asked. "You don't have that stomach flu that's going around, do you?"

Lori had obviously noticed something.

"I hope not. I'd hate to pass it on to my patients." Given the way word spread like wildfire around here, Nora added, "I'll take my temperature right away."

"Even if it's normal, you might want to wear a mask, just in case. But I don't suppose I have to tell you that."

"Thanks." After scrubbing her hands, Nora hurried out.

She was safe, for now. But the symptoms wouldn't go unnoticed for long.

Nora checked her watch. Lunchtime. She was debating whether to retrieve her sandwich or buy a salad at the hospital cafeteria when her cell rang.

The sight of Leo's name on the display gave her a happy-uneasy feeling. She didn't plan to tell him about her condition over the phone, of course, but what if she slipped? "Hi."

"Sorry for not calling sooner," he said. "And by the way,

I didn't mean to let my partner give you the bum's rush on Saturday."

Oh, no. Queasy again. At the end of the hallway, Nora perched on a window seat. "That's okay."

"I'm hoping you'll let me make up for it next Saturday, after we do whatever we're doing at the counseling center." When she didn't immediately answer, he added, "I can cook or we can eat out."

Please don't talk about food. Strange how she could be starving one minute and nauseated the next. "Fine either way."

"That's what's so great about you," Leo said. "You let life happen. I never feel like you're trying to box me into a corner."

This didn't bode well for the topic she had in mind. "I would never do that. But women do have to consider certain, well, long-term issues."

"Absolutely. And I'm glad you accept that I'm not the guy for that," he added cheerfully.

Through the window, Nora gazed toward the sea bluffs. Beyond seethed a sliver of blue ocean. Choppy surf. Ugh. She started to feel even more queasy. "Things do happen, things we don't plan."

"That's the best part, isn't it?" Leo sounded practically euphoric, probably anticipating another evening of spontaneous clothes tossing. "We have to be able to roll with the punches, right? And I do mean roll."

"Okay. I mean, right." She had to stop babbling and end this conversation, fast. "I'll see you Saturday and we'll, uh, plan to not make plans."

"Exactly."

Two seconds after they clicked off, Nora had no idea what they'd just agreed on. She was too busy barreling down the hall again.

Since her staff should have gone to lunch by now, she let herself into her private bathroom and took her time. If the nausea didn't get better soon, she might try acupressure. Several patients had reported good results with a nearby practitioner who specialized in women's conditions.

After she came out, she stiffened at a noise from another part of the suite. A moment later, she heard it again. A heavy sigh. Unless she'd been visited by an unusually moody burglar, it must be a staff member.

Nora popped in a breath mint and went to investigate.

At the nurse's station, Bailey sat propped on her elbows, staring at a line of photos pinned to the wall, photos of moms and babies brought in by patients. Her curly hair was mussed and her eyes shadowed. The nurse was clearly in distress.

Guiltily, Nora realized she'd been so absorbed in her own situation that she hadn't given much thought to the personal problems troubling Bailey. At twenty-eight, the nurse had always been energetic and self-sufficient. She told hilarious stories about the losers she dated, and had announced more than once she was glad other women had babies, because she doubted she'd ever want to.

Was it possible Bailey was pregnant, too? *Don't project onto her,* Nora warned herself. "What's wrong?"

"Oh!" Startled brown eyes met hers. "I thought you'd gone out."

"And came back." Nora pulled up a chair. "What's going on, if you don't mind my asking?"

Bailey released another long breath. "It's one of those ridiculous soap-opera situations I keep stumbling into."

"Another disappointing romance?" Untrustworthy men must give off subliminal signals that attracted vulnerable women like Bailey. And Nora, who had picked Reese and was now pregnant by a man who had Live Free or Die tattooed on his soul.

"It's my sister, Phyllis."

Shifting mental gears, Nora recalled Bailey mentioning an older half sister who was a financial counselor. "What's wrong?"

"She's had a series of miscarriages and she's hit a wall. She's so depressed."

Nora's heart went out to the woman. "Perhaps I could help. Or Dr. Tartikoff, when he gets here." Many causes of miscarriage, such as incompetent cervix or hormonal disorders, could be treated successfully.

The usually vibrant Bailey drooped like a two-day-old flower. "The fetuses had chromosomal abnormalities. Phyllis got tested and discovered she's the problem."

"Chromosomal rearrangement?" In 2 to 4 percent of repeated miscarriages, one of the parents turned out to have an inherited translocation of his or her chromosomes. This unusual structure didn't affect the parent but, because of the way chromosomes were passed from parent to child, could lead to the baby receiving extra or missing pieces of a chromosome.

A nod. "I'd never heard of it before. Now it seems like the most important thing in the world."

"She might still be able to have a healthy baby." While there was no cure for the condition, it didn't *always* result in an abnormal fetus. Sometimes the parents got lucky.

"She's miscarried five times, and she just turned forty."

Nora understood. "Has she considered adopting?"

"She and Boone want to be genetically related to their baby." Bailey's hands twisted together. "That's where I come in."

"You?" Nora frowned. "Oh! As an egg donor."

The nurse wrinkled her nose. "I offered. I even got tested

to make sure I don't have the same abnormality, which I don't. I guess I should have told you, but Phyllis insisted on confidentiality. I wouldn't be telling you now, but I have to talk to *someone*."

"About…?" Nora prompted.

"Phyllis and Boone asked me to be their surrogate. I mean, she's forty. It's too hard on her to keep going through this."

That raised a whole bunch of delicate issues. "Are you considering it?"

"I'd like to help. I'm actually curious about experiencing a pregnancy."

"What about when it comes time to give up the baby?" Nora asked.

Bailey shrugged. "That doesn't bother me so much, but since I'm the aunt, I can't avoid seeing how they're raising him or her. It might bother me if they don't do everything the way I would, which is hardly fair."

"You do believe they'll make good parents, don't you?"

Bailey studied the photos of babies arrayed before her. "I don't know. My parents were lousy role models, and Phyllis is so driven at work. It's all money, money, money. Of course that's good for me, since they've done a great job of investing my money." She'd been saving every spare dollar so she could study to be a nurse practitioner, able to treat patients herself for routine matters instead of assisting a doctor.

"You don't have to make a decision right away, do you?" Nora didn't see the hurry.

"When my sister makes up her mind, she's a force of nature." Then Bailey brightened. "Maybe I should talk to Mrs. Franco. She understands what it's like to be a surrogate."

"I'm sure she'd be happy to answer your questions. Keep in mind that things took an unusual turn for Kate." While Bailey must be aware that surrogates didn't normally get to keep the baby and marry the father, Kate and Tony's story was seductively romantic.

"I'll do that."

Nora's stomach churned, more from emptiness than anything else. Instinctively, she cupped a hand over her abdomen.

"You've got morning sickness, don't you?" Just like that, the tables turned and Bailey became the nurturer. "I knew you were anxious to have a baby even before that rat Reese did what he did. I don't blame you at all."

"Blame me?"

"Since you haven't mentioned seeing anyone, I figure you went the artificial route, right?"

"Well…" Nora tried to figure out how to reply.

"At another treatment center? Good idea," Bailey rambled on. "That's what I'd prefer, too. I'd rather keep my records private."

Doing a fast mental shuffle, Nora considered the explanation Bailey had provided. If people believed her pregnancy resulted from donor sperm, that would let Leo off the hook. He had a right to know the truth, but other people didn't need to find out.

Realizing her nurse expected a response, she seized on the last comment. "Our records *are* private." Patient confidentiality was taken very seriously in the medical profession.

"Anyone who works here can access the records," Bailey pointed out. "They shouldn't, but I'll bet they do if they get curious enough."

"That's grounds for firing. And possibly for legal action."

"Yeah, but you have to get caught first."

Nora heard the receptionist unlocking the door to the front office. "I guess we'd better table this conversation."

"Not another word." With a conspiratorial grin, the nurse departed.

Still reviewing the discussion, Nora went to her private office. Bailey had been right about one thing, for sure—the wisdom of keeping her medical records away from her colleagues at Safe Harbor. Just look at the way Dr. Tartikoff had gone hunting through Nora's infertility cases, presumably for the good of the patients, but in her opinion he'd had his own agenda.

An old friend and former fellow obstetrical resident, Dr. Paige Brennan, handled fertility cases along with her regular patients in Newport Beach, a few miles away. If Nora went to her, everyone would assume Dr. Brennan had done the insemination. And Paige was an excellent doctor.

Nora hadn't seen much of her former colleague recently, but in a way, that made it even better. For medical treatment, she preferred seeing someone who cared about her but wasn't emotionally invested in the details of her life.

As she downed a few bites of her sandwich before the first afternoon patient arrived, Nora wondered if she'd eventually have pursued artificial insemination on her own. Probably not. Without a man in the picture, it could be tough raising a child. Now she had no choice.

Leo was wonderful with his niece and nephew. Too bad…She stopped that line of thought. She couldn't yield to fantasies.

But where her sexy policeman was concerned, Nora found it hard not to.

Chapter Nine

Leo should have been enjoying the March sunshine, the chance to relax on his brother's patio and the sight of Tony and Kate frolicking in the pool with five-year-old Brady. Throw in the prospect of this evening with Nora, and everything ought to feel just about perfect on this rare free Saturday.

The problem was, he took his responsibilities seriously, even the ones that had nothing to do with his job.

"What do you think I should tell him?" he asked Tara, who sat propped in his lap drooling on a toy bunny. "I've been trying to remember what I was like at nineteen. Nothing like Ralph, I'm sure."

At that age, Leo had been studying criminal justice at Cal State Fullerton, not working at a supermarket. In some people's eyes, that would make Leo the more mature, responsible individual, but if he'd gotten a girl pregnant, he sure wouldn't have been agitating for marriage.

"By the time he's my age, he'd have a ten-year-old," Leo told his niece. "How weird would that be?"

"Da," she responded, or possibly, "Ba."

"Ba as in bunny?" he inquired.

She pressed her tiny lips together and batted her eyes at him. Flirting already, at this age.

"You're going to knock 'em dead by the time you're

three," Leo predicted. "Those preschoolers won't know what hit 'em."

"I hope you're giving her good advice," Tony called from the pool.

"She doesn't need good advice," Leo replied. "She has good parents."

And a great home to grow up in, he mused, taking in the hilltop view over the harbor. He imagined the parties she could throw as a teenager, with the outdoor kitchen and the meandering pool edged with rocks, ferns and a waterfall.

Leo resolved to give his own house a fresh coat of paint. That was the least he could do for... well, himself. Anyway, it wasn't the decor that made a home terrific. He'd grown up in a house as luxurious as Tony's, but he certainly hadn't experienced much happiness.

Tara burped, an outrageously loud noise for such a tiny baby. "Have you no manners?" Leo asked.

She gummed the bunny, happily unconcerned about etiquette.

For a moment, the sunlight dimmed as Leo pictured another Tara, the younger sister for whom his niece was named. Born with spina bifida, she'd had a restless mind and an outgoing personality trapped in a fragile body, and had died of pneumonia at the age of eleven. Devastated, his parents had retreated emotionally from their sons and each other.

Leo wondered if it had ever occurred to Ralph that parenthood might not be smooth sailing. At least that provided him with one good argument to present to the young man.

Wait. Wasn't he supposed to listen rather than lecture?

"What're you scowling about?" asked Kate as she and the others emerged, dripping, from the pool. His sister-in-law had a frank, open face, golden eyes and shoulder-length brown hair that looked a bit ragged around the edges, which was ironic considering her profession as a hairdresser.

"I am not looking forward to counseling a teenage boy." He'd mentioned the situation earlier, over brunch, without going into detail.

"You'll do fine. Trust your common sense." She draped a towel around her shoulders and turned to help Brady dry off.

"Trust my common sense? That's your advice?" Leo grumbled. "Not very inspiring."

Tony slid a damp arm around his wife. "She gives great advice. People come from far and wide to bask in her wisdom."

"One nurse, and she drove a mile." Kate rubbed a towel across her son's back "How about fixing Brady some hot cocoa?"

"Please, Daddy," the boy chimed in, and Tony beamed.

Leo knew his brother was thrilled that Brady had accepted him as his dad.

"Let's go see what we can scrounge up, okay?" Tony said.

Hand in hand, the pair went into the house. Kate lifted her daughter gently from Leo's lap. "Thanks for holding her."

He stretched his cramped legs. "Why is a nurse coming to you for guidance?"

"Her sister asked her to be a surrogate. She needed some insight into what's involved." His sister-in-law sat down on a straight chair beside his.

"What did you tell her?" Surrogacy had worked out well for Tony, but it hadn't been entirely smooth sailing.

"I encouraged her to explore her feelings and think about possible outcomes," Kate answered. "Although I was given a lot of information about the legalities involved, in retrospect, I was terribly naive."

That puzzled Leo. "Because you misjudged Esther's level of commitment?"

She tilted her face back to soak up the sunshine. "I also misjudged the impact on my family. My sister was very upset about the prospect of losing her niece, and it bothered my mom, too, even though she tried not to show it. As for me, it nearly tore me apart when the time came to give up the baby. I'm grateful I didn't have to."

He understood, up to a point. Still, the situation didn't seem that earth-shattering to him. "But if this woman's having a baby for her sister, she won't exactly be giving it away, right?"

"That could be even more painful, watching someone else raise her child." Kate caressed her baby's cheek. "Always feeling on the outside. Never hearing her call you mommy. I'm not sure this woman's come to terms with what it's going to mean for the rest of her life."

"Are we talking about Bailey?" Tony asked as he returned with his son and a mug of cocoa. The boy sat on the concrete and dumped out a bucket of Legos. A couple of pieces flew under Leo's chair and he nudged them back with his foot.

"No names," Kate warned her husband, and shifted Tara on her lap.

Tony looked rueful. "Sorry. I do know better. Not that she's likely to sue us, but a confidence is a confidence."

"Since I don't know her, the secret's safe with me." Leo recalled hearing about someone named Bailey, but he couldn't place the context. Besides, there had to be more than one woman with that name in Safe Harbor.

"Tell us more about this counseling you're doing,"

prompted his brother. "Much to our astonishment, I might add."

"Just talking to a kid I met while patrolling." Leo preferred to avoid mentioning Nora's involvement. As far as Tony and Kate knew, he'd driven her home after the reception, and that was the extent of their relationship.

The fewer people who nosed into his personal life, the better. That included his brother. Women seemed to thrive on heart-to-heart talks. To Leo, they felt intrusive.

However, he *could* use some insight into counseling Ralph, so he explained about the pregnant teen's insistence on giving her baby up for adoption, despite her boyfriend's objections. "Ultimately, it's her decision, right?"

"He could sue for the right to raise the child," said Tony, ever the lawyer. "He'd need to demonstrate to the court that he's capable of making a home and providing for the child alone. That would be tough, in view of his age."

"Single mothers do it all the time." Kate broke off to coo at the baby, who gurgled happily.

"Yes, but I don't think parenting comes as naturally to men," Tony countered. "Remember when you tried to prepare me for single fatherhood after Esther left? I was a wreck."

"You weren't that bad!"

"I suppose I'd have pulled it off with the help of a nanny. Not an ideal situation, though."

"This boy can't afford a nanny." Most working parents Leo knew used daycare centers. "Do people actually hire nannies around here? I thought that was more common in big cities."

"Professional people do. Don't you suppose that's what…a certain doctor has in mind when the baby comes?" Kate asked her husband.

"What doctor?" Leo wondered if he'd missed part of the conversation.

"The one Bail…the nurse works with," Kate said. "I suppose she shouldn't have told us about that."

"No, she shouldn't," Tony agreed. "Just as we shouldn't be discussing it in front of Leo."

"Absolutely not." Kate sighed. "But it's going to be common knowledge around the hospital soon enough."

While Leo hated having his own private business talked about, he liked to keep current on other people's affairs. Plus, he was still trying to get a fix on how to advise Ralph. "So this guy's planning to be a single father, too?"

"Which guy?" asked his brother.

"This doctor."

"*She* had artificial insemination." Kate jiggled Tara, who'd begun fussing. "Somebody's getting sleepy."

He was a she? Leo felt at sea in this conversation. "Maybe I should take a nap, too."

"What time's your appointment?" Tony got to his feet to help his wife gather the baby's gear. It sure took a lot of stuff—receiving blanket, pacifier, diaper bag—just to cart one infant up to the nursery.

"Not until…" Leo glanced at his watch. Almost half-past twelve. "One o'clock. Yikes." Just like that, his drowsiness vanished. There was nothing like a looming appointment to clear the mind.

As Leo took his leave and strode out to the car, he kept trying to make sense of the discussion. It felt as if he'd missed an important clue, but Leo couldn't figure out what.

Well, he had more important things to focus on. Such as how, with no experience whatsoever, he was going to help a teenage boy make good choices about becoming a father.

THE PAST FEW DAYS HAD BEEN hectic at Nora's office. Despite her desire to keep her pregnancy secret, word got out, probably because of her frequent trips to the bathroom and steady consumption of crackers and ginger ale. "Are you…?" was the most popular question of the week.

She gave Bailey permission to spread the explanation, which saved Nora from having to lie. Since she hadn't told people the story herself, that might make it easier to correct their false impressions later…if she decided to.

It all depended on how Leo reacted today. More than ever, Nora wished she'd told him last Saturday, but there simply hadn't been a chance.

Sure there was. Between the time you arrived at his house and when his partner showed up. But they'd been, well, preoccupied.

She'd love to get preoccupied again this afternoon. What were the ethics of taking a man to bed before giving him news that was likely to turn him into a stranger?

If the situation were reversed, she'd be furious. But Leo was a guy. Oh, man, was he ever.

She *had* to take her mind off him. It helped that when Nora arrived at the counseling center, she found it bursting at the seams. Eleanor and May Chong, the hospital's administrative secretary, had their heads together in the office. Judging by the snatches of conversation that reached Nora, they were applying for grants. The other room was occupied, as well. Through a glass panel, Nora could see Bailey talking intently with a thin-faced woman.

Suzy showed up at noon, and waved away a list of adoption attorneys that Nora had compiled. "I found a great lawyer right here in Safe Harbor. He says he has a couple who'll pay my living expenses and everything. I hope Officer Franco can talk sense to Ralph, because he needs to deal with it."

"Have you heard from Ralph this week?" Nora asked as they went outside to a grassy area furnished with a picnic table.

The girl piled her dark hair atop her head and then shook it free. "Nope. Getting questioned by the police must've scared him."

That seemed like a good sign. Nora hoped the young man intended to keep his appointment today, though. Ralph had a lot to work out. Dealing with him might be valuable for Leo, too, not that she had any illusions about him suffering a sudden onslaught of paternal feelings.

"How's your family taking all this?" Nora inquired.

"Oh, they're on Ralph's side. Nobody else in my family ever went to college, and they keep saying I shouldn't aim too high because I'll be disappointed. Like I *won't* be disappointed if I'm poor all my life!"

In response to Nora's questions, Suzy went on to describe her courses at the community college and her goal of transferring to the University of California to major in biology. The hour flew by as they discussed possible career paths, including medicine.

The girl got to her feet. "In case Ralph's coming, I'd better leave. It'll be easier if I avoid him."

Nora understood. "Would you like to meet again next week?"

Suzy looped her purse over her shoulder. "No, thanks. I've got everything under control."

"Give me a call if you ever want to talk." Nora handed her a card with her cell number.

"Thanks!" The girl breezed off.

She seemed more confident and organized than Nora felt about her own pregnancy. Wandering into the empty reception area, she almost wished she had someone to counsel *her*.

Since discovering she was pregnant, Nora had to admit she'd given only passing thought to how she was going to raise a child alone, or even to the reality of the small person growing inside her. Although she'd yearned for a baby, she found the ramifications so overwhelming that she'd mostly focused on what to tell Leo.

She'd never dreamed she'd become pregnant outside a committed relationship, or that she might have to consider how to handle a reluctant father. The problem wasn't so much that Leo might shrug off his responsibilities to their child, she realized. It was that she didn't want to lose this giddy, warm, hopeful feeling she experienced around him, or kill the joy in his eyes when he looked at her.

She couldn't be falling for the guy, could she? They were all wrong for each other. Outside the bedroom, they had practically nothing in common. Except that they always seemed to find plenty to talk about.

From the counseling room, Bailey emerged with her client. "Did you want to ask Dr. Kendall about a prescription to tide you over?" the nurse asked the woman, who clutched a sheaf of papers. Probably referrals and a list of resources.

At a guess, she might be in her mid-thirties, but she already had worry lines on her thin face. "I don't need a tranquilizer. Talking to you helped. I don't feel so hopeless now." The woman held out the papers. "I shouldn't take these."

"Keep them, in case you start feeling really down again."

"These moods, they're nothing I can't handle. I'll be fine once I get a job." The woman held on to the papers, though. After shaking hands with Bailey, she went out.

Despite an impulse to intervene, Nora held herself in check. Whether the woman suffered from depression or a less severe form of anxiety, she had the right to refuse treatment.

"How can you tell whether you're helping someone?" the nurse asked Nora when they were alone. "I'm not sure I deserve all the trust the clients put in me. I hear their sad stories and my life seems charmed by comparison."

While Bailey made her tales of disastrous dates and loser boyfriends sound funny, Nora knew real pain lay underneath. "Nobody's life is charmed. Besides, I'm sure you gave her good advice."

The nurse clicked her tongue. "Not really—more of a sympathetic ear. That's not much, considering she's got four kids to support and a husband in prison."

Eleanor and May were still murmuring together in the office. Nora kept her voice low. "Any further thoughts about the surrogacy?"

Bailey made a face. "My sister acts as if I've already agreed. She's picked some doctor in L.A. and she's urging me to go for my workup."

"There are issues you should discuss first." Surrogacy, even within a family, was never a simple matter. "I don't suppose she's mentioned compensation."

"Pay me? Phyllis?" Bailey snorted.

"Commercial surrogates earn upward of $25,000," Nora noted. "You'll have to take time off work, not to mention the discomfort and the physical risks. Your sister and her husband sound as if they're affluent. They should at least offer to pay you for the inconvenience and any lost wages."

"They won't. It's either the goodness of my heart or nothing."

"You also need a contract spelling out everyone's legal rights and obligations." Not only did the surrogate and the parents need to be protected, so did the child. Any number of factors could change during a pregnancy.

"Oh, she's had that drawn up. Down to the tiniest detail, I'll bet."

"Make sure you have your own attorney examine it." Nora felt obligated to point out another issue, as well. If she hadn't been so distracted by morning sickness, she'd have brought it up the first time Bailey broached the topic. "Usually surrogates have already given birth at least once. That's partly to reduce the risk of some undiagnosed medical condition surfacing, and also so they don't have to return home with empty arms."

"This isn't the same. I mean, it'll be my niece or nephew." Bailey seemed to be weighing in on the pro side.

"Well, don't rush." Nora's main concern was her nurse's tendency to be too trusting. Especially since Phyllis sounded domineering.

In the parking lot, a car cruised to a halt. Nora's pulse speeded as she glimpsed a flash of red through the open doorway. Leo's knock-your-eye-out sports car.

Bailey peered out, too. "Oh, my gosh, who is that hunk?"

"A friend of mine," Nora blurted.

Her nurse's eyebrows went up. Way up. "I didn't know you were seeing anyone."

She's perceptive, so watch it. "He's Tony Franco's brother. I persuaded him to counsel my client's boyfriend."

"Is he taken, or what?" Bailey asked. "I may seriously reconsider this whole surrogacy thing if that guy's on the loose."

For Bailey to go after Leo was the last thing Nora needed. "I have the impression he doesn't consider himself marriage material."

"In his case, a fling would be entirely acceptable." Bailey

smiled. "Relax. I'm not going to throw my sister under a bus for a casual affair. Still, I can hope he's one of those guys who find pregnant women sexy, can't I?"

"There's a name for men like that. They're called fathers." Nora stopped talking as Leo, all glorious six feet of him, cut along the pavement toward the center. When his gaze met hers, he unfurled a heart-stopping grin.

"Sorry I brought it up," Bailey murmured. "He doesn't even notice I'm alive."

Keenly aware that they were being watched, Nora restrained the impulse to greet Leo with a hug. "You're right on time," she told him.

His gray eyes swept her face. "You look great."

Don't stand here staring at each other. "You've heard me mention my nurse, Bailey," she said by way of introduction. "She's a volunteer here, also."

"Bailey?" Leo regarded the woman oddly. Not in a turned-on way, Nora was pleased to note, but as if he were trying to figure out how to fit a piece into a puzzle.

"What'd you think my name was?" the nurse asked.

"I didn't, um…" He broke off. "Nothing. Unimportant."

This waffling didn't seem like Leo. Uneasily, Nora noticed that he smelled like baby powder. "Were you over at your brother's?"

"For brunch," he confirmed.

Bailey's jaw dropped for an instant before she snapped it shut. What had she told the Francos? Nora wondered. And how much had they shared with Leo?

Before Nora could figure out how to raise the subject, she spotted Ralph loping toward them, skinny and angular, glasses sliding down his nose.

Compared to him, Leo looked mature and powerful. He

also looked a bit apprehensive. Clearly he'd been sweating what he was going to say to Ralph.

Their counseling session was about to begin. Nora would have to wait to find out what Leo had learned at his brother's house.

Chapter Ten

Bailey was Nora's nurse?

Striving to make sense of the bits and pieces, Leo replayed the conversation at his brother's house. A nurse named Bailey was considering becoming a surrogate mother, and the doctor she worked for had had artificial insemination.

Nora didn't look pregnant. Of course, having artificial insemination didn't always work. Nor did a woman necessarily become pregnant from a single encounter with an unprotected male.

An unprotected male... What was she doing, using him as backup?

The possibility rocked Leo. Now that he thought about it, the first time they met, Nora had commented on what a great father he'd make. He'd made it clear that he wasn't interested.

He hoped this pretty, loopy, delightful woman wasn't also manipulative and selfish. Surely not. Nothing about her character struck him as deceptive. More likely, he'd misunderstood the conversation at Tony's.

Meanwhile, here stood Ralph, wearing a backpack, baggy pants and an earnest expression. "I wasn't sure you'd come," the young man said.

"We made an appointment," Leo reminded him.

"People don't always keep their word."

Leo got that. "Granted. But I do."

Although he wasn't a great believer in coincidences, he put aside his questions about Nora and pregnancies. Hell, for all he knew, there might be two or three nurses named Bailey at Safe Harbor Medical Center. Perhaps the entire maternity ward was staffed by women named Bailey, Billie, Bambi and Betsy, who were frequently mistaken for each other, and all had doctors trying to get pregnant.

Yeah, right. Well, you never could tell.

"Let's go inside," he told Ralph, and left Bailey and Nora to sort out whatever they'd been discussing before his arrival.

Inside the counseling room, Ralph chose a seat at the table. Taking out his smart phone, he tapped some keys.

"What's this?" Leo pulled up a chair.

"My plan." The boy showed him a website on the screen. "See, I found these great sites for teen parents. Like this one. And this one." As he clicked from site to site, he outlined his goals for the immediate future.

It became apparent, as Ralph ran through the list, that the websites must be maintained by companies that manufactured baby gear, ran commercial day care centers and otherwise profited from young families. Nothing wrong with that, except for Ralph's unrealistic assumptions. According to him, the couple would acquire matching baby furniture, a huge array of educational toys and a ton of other baby equipment along with a spacious apartment to house it all. He also assumed Suzy could sign up the baby for day care as she pursued her education.

"How are you planning to pay for all this?" Leo asked.

"Oh, they take credit cards." Ralph flipped to another site. "Look at these educational computer programs for kids as young as three."

"Kids as young as three ought to be playing, not staring

at a screen," Leo told him. "And credit cards aren't free. If you don't pay off the balance you accumulate interest, plus I assume Suzy will have student loans."

"I hadn't thought about that." The boy's broad forehead creased. "But once she has her degree, she'll earn a lot, right?"

"A degree is a license to hunt. It gets you a shot at a better job or a promotion, but it's no guarantee of big bucks," Leo told him. "Especially when you're first starting out. Do you have medical insurance?"

"Not yet, but I'll qualify in another six months."

"What if the pregnancy's complicated?" He recalled the problems one of the dispatchers had had with her baby. "Or the child has special medical needs? Suppose Suzy gets pregnant again quickly, or decides she needs to pursue a master's degree?"

Ralph's jaw set stubbornly. "I can't worry about things like that."

How frustrating for Leo to see the potential problems looming ahead, while the young man clung to rosy dreams. Although he was tempted to lecture, Leo remembered that he was supposed to listen. "Tell me why you're so eager to take on a family at your age."

The boy clicked to a webpage displaying images of the world's cutest infants. Well, maybe not quite as cute as Tara, but almost. "Think about it. That's a part of me and Suzy growing inside her, and when it comes out, it'll be a whole new person." Another click, and toddlers replaced the newborns. "Walking. And talking! Imagine a little guy calling you Daddy."

The idea made Leo antsy. "Calling *you* Daddy, not me."

"Right. Me," Ralph agreed. "I mean, who am I? Some guy who's half Native-American and half nobody-knows-what, who got C's in high school and works at the supermarket. But to him, I'll be the most important man in the world."

Leo hadn't considered fatherhood in that light. "Ever worry that you might not live up to his expectations?"

Ralph bit his lips, which already looked well chewed. "Nobody's perfect. But I won't be like my dad, I can tell you that.'

"The one who ran out."

"Or my stepdad, who used to hit my mom. That was my first stepdad. The second one was a drunk who smashed up his car and bled to death."

"Great role models," Leo muttered.

"Actually, they were—role models for what I'm not going to be," Ralph said fiercely.

The kid had courage and determination. "You *will* be a good father. The problem is, I'm not sure Suzy's ready to be a mother."

"We'll work it out." Ralph stuck the phone back in his pocket.

Leo had run out of questions, and he certainly didn't have any further advice. "Anything else I can do?"

"I'll ask Suzy if her parents' policy will cover her pregnancy." The young man tilted his head as he considered. "Maybe we don't need all those diaper stackers and stuff, either."

"You could check out thrift stores." The dispatcher at the department had raved about her terrific finds at Goodwill.

"Yeah. It isn't material things that matter, anyway. It's the people you love." The boy stood and shook hands with Leo. In this lean youth with remnants of teenage acne, Leo saw the makings of a stern but loving father. He could picture Ralph at forty, guiding his teenagers through their tough decisions.

The kid had potential. He wondered whether Suzy appreciated that.

"I'm not sure I've been much help, but if you'd like to meet again, I'd be happy to," Leo said.

"Great. Next Saturday?"

Leo had an early shift, but it turned out Ralph could come at four. The boy seemed pleased that they'd be meeting again. Maybe Leo hadn't entirely wasted their time.

In the outer office, there was no sign of Bailey, but two other women had joined Nora. The newcomers were physical opposites, one tall and patrician with silvering hair, the other a short Chinese woman. After Ralph left, Nora introduced them as the center's volunteer director, Eleanor Wycliff, and the hospital's administrative secretary, May Chong.

"You met her son, Ted, last week," Nora explained after they'd exchanged greetings. "He's picking May up in a few minutes."

"We're lucky to have Ted as a volunteer," Eleanor said. "Something's always going wrong with computers."

May smiled. "He's a good boy."

"Where does he work?" Leo asked.

"He runs his own consulting business."

"Good for him." It seemed the polite thing to say, although Leo had no idea whether Ted's consulting business enabled him to earn a living.

"He's very ambitious."

Enough chitchat. Leo wished Ted would show up to collect his mother and Eleanor would go about her business. Talking to Ralph about babies had, if anything, intensified his curiosity about Nora. How could a guy tell if a woman was pregnant, anyway?

He'd heard that one of the first signs was fuller breasts, so he sneaked a glance at her chest, which was pretty much what he wanted to do, anyway. A green jersey top clung suggestively to her form. *Were* her breasts bigger than he remembered, and how soon could he find out up close and personal?

"You had some suggestions regarding security?" Eleanor inquired, cutting off this tantalizing line of speculation. "Dr. Forrest isn't here, but you can fill me in and I'll take notes for her."

"Yes, of course." It appeared his detective work was going to have to wait a bit longer. Leo hoped she hadn't noticed him ogling.

May decided to stand out front to watch for her son. As for Nora, she waved to a dark-haired young woman approaching across the parking lot. Violet Nguyen. Back for another counseling session, apparently.

"Sorry to miss your security briefing," Nora said.

"I'll be glad to review it with you later," Leo murmured, and spotted a glint of appreciation in Eleanor's expression. Obviously, she'd picked up on their connection. Well, so what? He was only human.

As for Nora, a blush was all the answer she gave before escorting Violet into the counseling room. From a side angle, her bust definitely looked bigger. On the other hand, that might be his imagination.

"We're lucky to have an obstetrician as a counselor," the older woman told Leo. The front room felt echoingly empty with only the two of them present.

For a fleeting second, he considered asking Eleanor if she'd heard anything about Nora's plans to have a baby. That would be too obvious, not to mention indiscreet. "Well, let's start with always having two or more staff members on the premises and making sure someone keeps an eye on the door," he said.

From her pocket, Eleanor retrieved a half-dozen business cards. "Good idea. Someone keeps leaving these, and

I've never been able to figure out who. This center doesn't promote private services."

Leo glanced at the cards. Fergus Bridger, Attorney at Law, Specializing in Adoptions. "You might call him to ask."

"It's hardly important enough to bother with," the director said. "The truth is, we get salespeople pushing all sorts of things in here all the time."

"Some of them could be thieves, scouting for items worth stealing. You should ask everyone who comes in for ID. That way, if something's missing, we'll know where to start."

Leo ran through his other points. Mostly common-sense items like locking the exterior door when no one was available to keep an eye on it, and making sure someone in the main building knew what time the key should be dropped off. Eleanor took notes and asked intelligent questions.

Leo appreciated her thoroughness, because he wanted to keep these people safe. One of them in particular.

NORA HADN'T RECEIVED MUCH satisfaction from Bailey. The nurse had admitted she'd yammered freely to Kate, but wasn't sure exactly how much she'd disclosed about Nora. "I certainly didn't *mean* to tell her anything about your private medical business."

"You shouldn't have mentioned me at all." Nora disliked scolding her nurse, who looked very repentant, but she really was irked. What an awkward way for Leo to learn…whatever he'd learned.

"You like this guy, don't you?" Bailey asked. "You think he'll dump you because you got inseminated?"

"There's nothing serious between us." *Please don't probe further.*

Finally, Bailey had left Nora to make polite conversation with Eleanor and May, and then with Leo. Did he really keep sneaking glances at her breasts, right in front of the others? The guy was shameless. And adorable.

Or did he suspect something? She hated this whole business of keeping secrets. They seriously needed to clear the air, the sooner the better.

For now, though, she faced the young woman sitting tensely on the faded love seat and drew out a list of resources. "I've done some research into legal aid."

"I don't want charity," Violet insisted.

"It isn't charity. Many lawyers donate time—they call it working pro bono, for the public good—because helping people is one of the reasons they chose their profession." Nora handed her the paper. "The baby's father has legal obligations. He's over eighteen, isn't he?"

Violet accepted the list as if it burned her fingers. "Yes."

Perhaps a less touchy subject would break the ice. "How did you meet him?"

"In high school." Tautly, Violet added, "His parents don't like me."

"Because you're from a different background?" Nora guessed.

The girl laced her fingers across her large abdomen. "Yes. They're rich and my mom runs a flower shop. Also, we're Vietnamese and they're white."

"Is your father in the picture?" Nora knew better than to assume young people had two parents at home.

"He died five years ago. Lung cancer. He smoked a lot." Violet stared down at her hands.

She seemed even more tightly wound today than the previous Saturday. "What happened this week to upset you?" Nora asked impulsively.

Violet blinked. "I, uh, phoned Gary."

"The father?"

A nod.

"And?"

In the silence that followed, she heard Eleanor addressing Leo in the other room. Something about having to be careful not to scare off the clients.

"He called me names."

"He won't help you, I take it." Nora felt an urge to shake the young man.

The girl swallowed. "No, and then he…" She came to a dead stop.

"Did he threaten or hit you?" Nora prompted. "We can talk to Officer Franco if you like."

Violet stared at the floor. "If I ask his opinion, does he have to do anything about it?"

Nora weighed her response. She didn't believe in giving false assurances, but neither did she wish to discourage Violet from reporting a possible crime. "That depends on what you tell him, but I'm certain he'll take your wishes into account."

"Do you trust him?" the girl asked.

Nora did, absolutely. Still, if the boy was truly dangerous, she knew that law enforcement couldn't always protect the victim. "Did Gary assault you?"

"No." Violet cleared her throat. "Let's talk to the policeman."

"Okay." As they walked out, Nora hoped Leo could help. Her own problems seemed minor in comparison to this frightened girl's.

Sometimes it took a reality check to put your own life into perspective.

Chapter Eleven

Leo caught Nora's warning gaze. This must be a serious matter, as if he hadn't already grasped that from the way Violet kept wringing her hands.

"She has something to discuss with us," Nora said, as if they were all in this together. Whatever "this" might be.

"Sure." Since Eleanor was in her office with the door closed, Leo offered them both seats in the waiting area. "What's going on?"

Violet heaved a couple of long breaths, clearly working up her nerve. Gently, Nora started the discussion for her. "Violet talked to her ex-boyfriend about supporting the baby, but he refused."

"This was in person or by phone?" Leo liked to get the whole picture.

"By phone." Violet lifted her chin. "He hung up on me. Then he emailed my mother and threatened her."

Mentally, Leo switched gears from friendly counselor to police officer. He took out a small pad he always carried. "What kind of threats?"

"That if I don't give up my baby, he'll hurt her business. Spread rumors that she sends poor-quality flowers."

While blackmail was illegal, something so general might not quite rise to the level of a crime. "Did he threaten anything more specific? Arson, perhaps?"

Violet's mouth opened in dismay. "Oh, no. Of course not."

Still, the threats could escalate. Better track them down before that happened. "Did he send these emails from his own account and put his name on them?"

"My mother said he didn't sign his name. Too big a coward. I don't know what account he used," the girl admitted. "My mom is very upset. She threatened to kick me out unless I go to an adoption attorney."

Nora laid a reassuring hand on the teenager's arm. "If you need a place to stay, I'll help you find one. "

Leo still felt he hadn't grasped the whole story. "Was he specific about how he planned to spread the rumors? Via internet, or word of mouth? Unless your ex-boyfriend has a business that orders a lot of flowers, I'm not sure why anyone would believe him."

"It isn't him, it's his parents. The Hightowers. People would believe *them*," she finished unhappily.

Now the picture came into focus. "Your boyfriend is Roy Hightower's son?"

Violet nodded. "His name's Gary."

"It's hard to believe the Hightowers would be involved in something like this."

"The name sounds familiar," Nora said. "Roy Hightower's on the city council, isn't he?"

"That's right. He and his wife were at my brother's wedding." While Leo didn't particularly like them, he couldn't picture the couple stooping this low.

"They hate me." Violet's voice shook. "They don't want anything to do with their own grandchild."

Spreading rumors sounded like something a boy might do, but not his parents, no matter how much they disapproved of the relationship. Leo was reluctant to stir up trouble with a family that might be innocent.

Especially when they're important people who could screw up your promotion?

He couldn't let that consideration affect his judgment. "I'd like to see those emails. Let's pay your mother a visit."

The girl took a deep breath. "She's at the shop. Saturday's a busy day. If I scare the customers, she'll be furious."

"This isn't an official police inquiry." Leo's gesture took in his jeans and work shirt. "Dr. Kendall and I just want to…"

While he searched for an appropriate phrase, Nora said, "Nip this in the bud."

Violet groaned. "Flower puns?"

Nora laughed. "That wasn't intentional."

"It's okay." The girl seemed to relax, perhaps because she now had a couple of grown-ups on her side. "My mom's name is Rose and mine is Violet, so we're used to it."

She gave them an address for Rose's Posies on Safe Harbor Boulevard, not far from the hospital. Leo recalled seeing the sign; he'd probably driven past it hundreds of times. "We'll meet you there."

Outside the counseling center, they found Ted Chong talking intently with his mother. The young man's face brightened when he spotted Violet. "Well, hello again. How're you doing?"

"Okay. Thanks for asking." She gave him a shy smile.

May patted Violet's bulge. The contact seemed presumptuous to Leo, but the teen didn't appear to mind. "Boy or girl?"

"It's a girl."

May clicked her tongue sympathetically. "Daughters are expensive to raise, always wanting new clothes."

"Sons are expensive to raise, too," Ted joked.

His mother gave his head a playful smack, ruffling his straight, black hair. "Yes, just look at you."

He dodged away, then pushed his glasses into place. "Okay, Mom. Let's get going. Violet, lots of luck. I like the photos on your Facebook page. Let me know if you need anything."

"Thanks."

Leo found it hard to believe the guy might be romantically interested in a girl about to give birth to another guy's baby. He was probably just being kind.

To his relief, Nora didn't argue about riding in Leo's car and leaving hers at the center. Finally, they had a private moment, he mused as they zipped out of the parking lot.

Too bad it was such a short drive. He'd better not waste any time.

"I was wondering about your nurse," he said.

"Bailey? She thinks you're cute, by the way." Nora leaned back in her seat. He liked the way her skirt played over her knees and the fabric of her top touched her chest lightly. Nothing cheap or overdone about her, yet she exuded sensuality.

Large breasts. For once, they made him think about something *other* than sex. "That's not what I meant." How was he going to put this? "At my brother's this morning, my sister-in-law mentioned a nurse named Bailey."

"Did the word *surrogate* come up?" Nora asked.

"It did."

The sports car crawled along Ocean View Avenue. Ordinarily, Leo never drove this slowly except on patrol or in a school zone.

"Was that followed by a discussion of anything else?" Nora asked.

He'd better get to the point, because there was never a traffic jam when you needed one. In fact, there was no traffic at all today. "Are you trying to get pregnant?"

"Not exactly." She seemed to be staring everywhere but at him.

"How do you *not exactly* try to get pregnant?" The last thing he wanted was to conduct an interrogation, especially with her seductive perfume tickling his libido, but it was time to get this out in the open. "If you want to have artificial insemination, that's your business. What bothers me is the idea of being manipulated. Used."

"That isn't the problem." Nora still failed to meet his gaze.

"Well, what *is* the problem?" he returned, irritated at her ambiguity.

"The problem is, I wasn't trying to get pregnant," she said, "but I am."

NORA DESPERATELY WISHED SHE could read Leo's expression. He simply stared straight ahead without speaking, and before she could query him, they reached the parking lot of Rose's Posies. There stood Violet, waving at them.

Nora wished she didn't feel so guilty. Sure, Leo had jumped into bed without taking precautions, just as she had. But she was an ob-gyn, for heaven's sake. And she was well aware that men in heat didn't always think with their brains.

She felt as if she'd let him down. And herself, too. This relationship had started to mean far more than she'd ever intended. She still found Leo's nearness utterly distracting. She kept itching to tangle her legs around his—a bad idea, particularly while he was driving—and to run her palm across his cheek to feel that careless Saturday stubble.

Would they ever be intimate again? Or was this the sad end to a sweetly unforgettable episode? One she was going to be reminded of every time she gazed into her child's face.

Whatever his opinions, Leo kept them well hidden as he

tucked his car deftly into an undersize space. Rose's Posies was nestled amid a row of older stores with a cramped parking area that would never win approval from the current city powers. The lot was further truncated by the presence of a refrigerated delivery truck into which a wizened old man was loading bouquets.

Violet led them inside, past storage shelves of vases, baskets and supplies, then a series of refrigerated cases filled with flowers, and finally into a small, charming shop that overflowed with teddy bears, shiny plants and racks of gifts. The scent of vanilla wafted from an array of candles.

At a round table, two women similar enough to be mother and daughter pored over photo books of arrangements. Judging by the white lacy trim on the covers, Nora guessed them to be wedding arrangements.

"There you are!" A small Vietnamese woman poked her head over the counter, which was almost tall enough to hide her. "Violet, go and help Mr. Tran with the deliveries."

Her daughter didn't budge. "I brought some people to see you."

Her mother regarded them uncertainly. "Customers?"

"No. Friends."

"No friends during business hours!"

"Mrs. Nguyen?" Leo spoke in a low tone. "May we speak with you privately?"

"Who are you?" the woman demanded.

"He's a cop, Mom," Violet declared. "He's here about the threats."

The women at the table stopped debating the merits of carnations vs. miniature roses and glanced up.

"You don't look like a cop," Rose said.

He produced his badge. "I'm Leo Franco and this is Dr. Nora Kendall. We're volunteer counselors at the Edward

Serra Memorial Clinic. We just want to ask you about a few things."

"What things?" she demanded.

Violet planted her hands on her hips. "The emails, Mom."

"May I see them?" Leo asked.

"I deleted them." Her mother shook her head in annoyance. "It's nothing. My daughter likes to make trouble."

"I'm not here in an official capacity, but I will be glad to file a report if you're concerned," he continued levelly.

"That's all I need, to insult a city councilman's son!" The florist glared at her daughter. "You brought it on yourself, getting involved with a boy like that. You should do the right thing and give up the baby."

"I am doing the right thing," Violet responded heatedly. "I'm taking care of your granddaughter."

The customers at the table exchanged glances. The younger one started to get up but her mother touched her arm, and she settled down again. However, Nora feared that any further arguing might drive them both away.

"We really should talk in private," she told Violet's mother.

The florist folded her arms. "We have no problems here."

Leo handed her his business card. "If you receive any further emails or threats of any kind, please save them for me. Call right away if there's anything serious."

Reluctantly, Rose pocketed the card, then caught her daughter's elbow possessively. "Very nice to meet you people," she told Leo and Nora.

Clearly, they'd been dismissed. There was nothing else they could do, Nora reflected as they took a polite leave. Perhaps nothing else they *should* do.

"You don't suppose this boy, Gary, will actually try to harm them, do you?" she asked as they got into Leo's car.

"Let me put it this way. People will do surprisingly stupid things, so we can't discount the possibility. However, a vague threat to spread rumors about Violet's mother's business probably just reflects the guy's frustration about the pregnancy." He shot the car into Reverse so fast Nora had to grab the handgrip. "Seems to be a lot of that going around."

"Pregnancy or frustration?"

"Both."

What had she expected, three cheers and a diamond ring? "Leo, I didn't plan this."

"Then what was that business about artificial insemination?"

"A smoke screen. I had to tell Bailey something." When he didn't respond, she went on. "She's an obstetrical nurse and it's no surprise she noticed my morning sickness. Would you rather I announced that you knocked me up?"

He was driving fast, in contrast to his snail's pace on the way over. "You're saying that you didn't intentionally treat me like a stud?"

A stud? "Oh, get over yourself!"

Leo started to laugh but cleared his throat instead. "You're a doctor. I thought you were on the pill, or used some other kind of birth control."

"I wasn't sleeping with anyone and I didn't plan to," Nora shot back. She hated arguing. "Look, I'm not asking you for anything, okay? No money. No involvement if that's what you prefer. We can let people think I got pregnant in a fertility clinic. I've arranged to see a doctor in Newport, so my coworkers won't have access to my records."

That ought to satisfy him. But he continued glowering.

"You think that squares it?" The words emerged ragged.

"You're carrying my son or daughter, and I'm supposed to just walk away? It doesn't work like that, Nora."

It did for some people. But not for a good man like this one, she reflected, and felt worse than ever. "This puts you in a bind, huh? For me, it wasn't intentional, but I do want a child. Maybe you will someday."

Someday when he was emotionally ready. *And finds the right woman,* added a cruel voice in her head.

"Maybe, but not now."

They pulled alongside her car, which in their absence had become surrounded by other vehicles. People were making their way on foot toward the community center entrance, above which hung a banner: "Free Tax Help 4:00-6:00 p.m. Saturday."

Next year, she'd have a new dependent to list. *But I'll still be filing solo,* Nora reflected glumly.

She tried to find something else to say. A joke about missing their dinner together died unvoiced. Finally she mumbled, "I'm sorry," and then got annoyed, because she was no more at fault than he was.

"Me, too," he said.

After she exited, he waited until she got in her car and started the engine. Ever the gentleman.

Then his car vroomed off, disappearing among the vehicles of help-seeking taxpayers. "Well," Nora said aloud as she backed out, "that could have gone worse."

But she wasn't sure how.

Chapter Twelve

After a restless weekend, Leo took satisfaction in the orderly familiarity of the police station on Monday morning. Here, at least, he could focus on external issues and escape troubling uncertainties.

That illusion lasted until the captain stopped him outside the locker room. "See me after briefing." Without waiting for a reply, Reed walked off.

"You in the doghouse?" asked Patty, who'd witnessed the exchange.

Mentally Leo replayed his recent activities, but nothing sprang to mind as a problem. "No idea."

Half an hour later, after taking notes about a bank robber working the area, a hit-and-run vehicle to watch for and a pack of stray dogs that had trashed the mayor's yard and scared the bejeebers out of his cat, Leo trudged up the stairs to the detective bureau.

Nearly every desk was staffed as detectives prepared for the week. A couple of guys wore ties and a woman in Juvies had put on a skirt and pumps, signs that they were due in court to testify.

That was what Leo craved. His own cases to handle and follow through to conviction. Further down the line, a chance to move up. He'd like to be chief of a place like this someday.

He found the captain's door open. After a quick knock, Leo went in.

"Have a seat." Reed studied a sheet of paper covered with handwritten notes too messy to make out, even if Leo could read upside down and without getting caught.

"The chief received an interesting call at home yesterday," Reed said, and gazed at him coolly.

Being clueless, Leo had no trouble keeping his own expression blank.

"From City Councilman Roy Hightower," the captain went on. "Ring a bell?"

"I'm acquainted with him, yes." His mind raced. That scene in the flower shop on Saturday... While names had been mentioned, nothing had come of it. Leo hadn't even been on duty.

"The chief promptly relayed the subject of this call to me. On a Sunday." The captain didn't sound happy about being disturbed at home. "It seems, if I understand this correctly, that his son's pregnant girlfriend claims you're investigating the family about some threats to a flower shop. Councilman Hightower contends no such threats were made."

Oh, great. Leo had volunteered to help the girl and she'd squawked like a chicken. What was that quote about no good deed going unpunished? "The young lady would be Miss Violet Nguyen, I presume."

"That sounds about right." Reed sat, waiting.

Leo struggled to organize his thoughts. "She's a client at the counseling center. On Saturday, she asked Dr. Kendall and me to talk to her mother about some anonymous emails urging that Violet relinquish her baby for adoption. The girl believes her boyfriend, Gary Hightower, was behind them, but Mrs. Nguyen had deleted the emails. The threats were vague, and there's no way to tell who sent them. Since Mrs.

Nguyen wanted the matter dropped, it went no further. I was off duty at the time," he added.

"Did you contact the boy or his family?"

"No, sir," Leo said.

"Did you file a report?"

"I saw no reason for one. I did stop by and mention it to the watch commander, but he didn't seem to think it important." Leo considered it wise to keep his superiors informed.

The captain drummed his fingers on the desk. "How's the counseling going, by the way? You mentioned a young man. That's not Gary Hightower, is it?"

"No, sir." Leo didn't elaborate further. Although no one had lectured him about confidentiality, to him it went without saying.

"So, have you seen this fellow again?"

Strange question, but Leo didn't want to appear defensive. "We met on Saturday, before I learned about Miss Nguyen's concerns. I'd say the session went well."

The captain watched him expectantly, as if curious to see what else might fall out of Leo's mouth. Obviously, Reed had mastered the interrogation technique of letting silence loosen a person's tongue. The fact that Leo's promotion was on the line added to the pressure.

Despite the temptation to defend himself or yak about the merits of his volunteer work, Leo kept his mouth shut. Anything he said would more likely hurt than help.

The captain broke the silence first. "Did you present your security recommendations to the staff?"

"Yes, sir." Leo summarized his talk with Eleanor Wycliff.

After he finished, the captain's expression remained impassive. "Do you plan to continue volunteering there?"

"I scheduled another counseling session for next Saturday." In all honesty, Leo added, "It's not as if I have parenting experience. But the boy grew up without a father and he appears to value masculine feedback."

A slow nod. "I can understand that." The captain, long divorced, had a son in the army and another in college, Leo recalled. "Well, let me know if these threats escalate."

"I'll do that, sir."

On his way out, Leo noted Mike Aaron paying him particular attention. From the corner of his eye, he also spotted Trent Horner emerging from the sergeant's office and regarding him with a smirk.

Much as he liked helping at the counseling center, Leo'd never intended for his volunteer work to get in the way of his job. Moreover, being around Nora seemed to affect his judgment, and not in a good way.

Once they resolved this business about how they were going to deal with the baby, he had to distance himself from her and everything concerning her. And the sooner he got that over with, the better.

STAYING UP ALL NIGHT WAS a lot harder at thirty-four than when she'd been in med school in her twenties, Nora reflected early Monday morning. Hold on—she checked the date on her watch—how could she have lost track of the dates? It was her birthday. She was thirty-five today.

Maybe that explained why her eyes felt like they were developing permanent bags and her feet hurt despite the sensible shoes. Being pregnant didn't help, either.

Happy birthday, Mommy.

She tried to avoid her tired reflection in the window of the nursery as she gazed over the rows of newborns. Four of them had come into the world last night. The first face they'd seen was hers.

Amazing to think that her womb carried a new life also,

a tiny person nestled tightly inside, too small for her to feel its movements. Yet someday that baby would grow large enough to hold in her arms, utterly loving and totally dependent on Nora to shelter, guide and love him or her.

Tears pricked Nora's eyes as she remembered the distress on Leo's face when she broke the news. Too bad he wasn't willing to share this joy with her.

He hadn't dismissed the subject and walked away, despite her willingness to let him. The man had a conscience. She also suspected he had a heart, but for whatever reason, it didn't belong to her.

She had to stop this mental whining. Maternal hormones had been wreaking havoc with her emotions all weekend.

Well, she had precious little time to grab breakfast, change into the spare set of clothes she kept handy and prepare to see patients. Reminding herself that she *had* managed to grab a few hours of sleep in the on-call room between deliveries, Nora squared her shoulders and headed downstairs to the cafeteria.

On the ground floor, it sounded as if someone was drilling for oil in the basement. This construction ruckus couldn't be good for the patients' health, but Nora knew it was unavoidable.

With no temptation to linger over breakfast, she managed to complete her tasks and emerge from her private bathroom with twenty minutes to spare. Only then did she notice how unusually quiet it was. The short hallway between her office and the nurses' station lay deserted. What was going on?

"Surprise!" Out of the examining rooms popped Bailey, the receptionist and the billing-and-records clerks.

Mark Rayburn stepped from an alcove. "Happy birthday."

"Cake," Bailey added, gesturing toward the nurses' station.

There stood a splendid pink cake topped with cherries. Nora's favorite. "I had no idea you were planning this."

The staff burst into a rousing chorus of "Happy Birthday." Bailey hammed up the ending with "and many many many many more!"

"I know you were on call last night," Mark said. "Seems unfair on your birthday, but I certainly appreciate it. We wanted to perk you up with a celebration."

"You're all so sweet." She felt teary again, this time in a happy way. So many friends, chattering and cutting slices. The cake was delicious, and never mind that she'd already eaten. Too bad she couldn't enjoy a cup of coffee with it.

No one mentioned her pregnancy, but she caught the curious glances aimed at her midsection. "Okay," Nora said finally. "Since you're all wondering, yes, we do have something extra to celebrate. I'm due in November."

Applause broke out. She'd already told Mark privately but he smiled as broadly as the others. Since patients must be arriving in the waiting room by now, she waved for quiet. "I'm not sure I want to broadcast this far and wide."

"Mum's the word," said Bailey.

Considering how much the nurse had already blabbed to the Francos, that wasn't reassuring. Well, so what? Nora might be a single mom, but she wasn't completely alone.

Definitely not alone, she learned later that morning, when Bailey conceded quietly that she'd decided to yield to her sister's request. "I'll be a few months behind you, but pregnancy loves company, right?" the nurse said.

"In my case, definitely."

Nora switched gears to prepare for her next patient, Una Barker. With her husband, Jim, she had been undergoing fertility treatments at a modest pace to suit their budget. A personal memo from Dr. Tartikoff had urged Nora to pursue more advanced procedures for them. But, although she occasionally reminded them of their options, Nora would only bring up the subject again if it seemed appropriate. No hotshot fertility director's agenda was going to affect her practice of medicine.

To her surprise, she found Una wearing a flattering turquoise dress rather than the usual hospital gown. Heavyset and stylish, with animated features, she sat in the chair usually occupied by her husband.

"I've stopped taking the hormones," Una told Nora after they exchanged greetings. "Jim and I have decided to adopt."

"That's wonderful news." As she spoke, Nora tried to sort out her reaction. Had she failed them? Perhaps Dr. Tartikoff was right, and she should have pursued high-tech solutions more aggressively. "I didn't realize you wanted to stop treatments."

Una stretched languorously. She seemed much more relaxed than usual. "Out of the blue, we got a call from an attorney who specializes in adoptions. I'm not sure where he found our number, but he's local, and he has several young mothers giving birth in the next month. I want a baby now. I'm tired of all these ups and downs."

Trying to conceive was hard on patients, Nora understood. Each month, hope rose anew, only to be dashed when the woman's period arrived.

However, adoption wasn't necessarily an easy course, either. "You realize that an adoption isn't guaranteed until the mother signs the final papers. It can be heartbreaking to take a baby home and have to give it back."

"This lawyer says he's had a lot of success," Una told her. "And since the mother's due very soon, we won't have long to wait."

"I hope no one's taking advantage of you financially." That was the most diplomatic phrasing Nora could muster.

"Since it's illegal to buy and sell babies, any money you provide to assist the birth mother is hers to keep, even if she changes her mind."

"I know it's a risk, but my in-laws are willing to help out financially," the woman said. "My instincts tell me it's the right decision, Dr. Kendall. I hope you aren't disappointed in us."

"Disappointed?" Nora hadn't considered that her patient might worry about *her* feelings. "Not at all. I'm thrilled for you. I hope you'll let me know how this works out. Please bring the baby for a visit."

"I'd love to." After a little more discussion, they shook hands, and Nora held the door for her patient.

As she updated her notes in the computer, she tried to pinpoint the cause of her uneasiness. She didn't care how Dr. Tartikoff might react to her losing a fertility patient. And she understood why Una was eager for the chance to start parenting and put this painful struggle behind her.

Then it hit her. A few weeks ago, another couple, the Arrigos, had told her almost the same story. The pair, who objected to in vitro fertilization for religious reasons, had heard from a local adoption attorney about the availability of an infant scheduled to be born in a few weeks. It was probably a coincidence, but where *had* he obtained their phone numbers?

Nora wished she'd asked whether Una had signed up on any fertility-related websites. That might explain it.

No one was being coerced, she reminded herself. This wasn't a crime. And she would never throw a wrench into Una's happiness. Given the ridiculous ease with which Nora had conceived, that would be hypocritical.

All the same, she wished she could discuss the situation with Leo. Cold, hard common sense told her their future conversations would probably be limited to his financial contribution to their child's care.

A knot formed in Nora's gut. How could she care so much for a man who was obviously wrong for her? Or, more accurately, for whom *she* was obviously wrong. Younger, strikingly handsome and radiating masculinity, Leo belonged with one of those confident women she'd watched in awe and envy all her life. A woman who'd always felt beautiful, who knew that she deserved the best and wasn't afraid to take it.

Not that Nora undervalued herself. Guys found her attractive, and she'd worked hard to earn success as a doctor. But she and Leo had been meant to be two ships that pass in the night or, rather, that pass on by after a couple of pleasurable nights.

Now she had to drum that fact into her uncooperative brain.

A churning stomach and the need to concentrate on her patients kept Nora's mind occupied through the morning. Then a pregnant patient came in without an appointment to discuss a concern about spotting, and a prospective patient requested a few minutes to get to know Nora. She ended up grabbing lunch at her desk, along with a second slice of the rapidly vanishing birthday cake, and stayed until the last patient left at five-thirty.

"Big plans for tonight?" asked Bailey as Nora headed for the exit.

"Big plans to catch up on my sleep," she admitted.

The nurse clasped her hands nervously. "Is it okay if I take Thursday morning off? My sister made an appointment with a doctor in L.A. for my initial workup."

"Of course." Nora scheduled surgeries for Tuesday and Thursday mornings, and was assisted by a surgical nurse at the hospital, so she wouldn't need Bailey until the afternoon anyway. "Good luck."

Bailey's nose wrinkled. "I'm not looking forward to monitoring my cycle and all that stuff. Let's pray I get pregnant fast."

"Absolutely." While Nora wasn't sure her nurse had truly considered all the angles, there was no sense in harping on her doubts.

As she let herself into the hallway, her thoughts returned to her milestone birthday. Her father hardly ever remembered birthdays on time. Growing up, Nora had accepted birthday cakes purchased hurriedly from the supermarket and gifts in the form of cash as normal celebrations that came a week or a month late. But she'd always known that her father loved her deeply.

Well, today she should treat herself to a special present. Since her favorite pastime was reading, the prospect of a stop at Fact and Fiction, Safe Harbor's independent bookstore, quickened her step.

In her peripheral vision she caught movement to the left and an impression of a couple emerging from Dr. Rayburn's office. The sound of their bickering put Nora on edge.

Then she recognized a voice she knew intimately. Reese was saying, "I told the cook we'd be eating at home. She's gone to a lot of trouble to fix what the nutritionist suggested."

"I'm tired of rabbit food." Could this be slender, elegant Persia? The hair was still glossy and black, but her cheeks looked puffy and her jawline sagged. Even considering the pregnancy, she'd gained a lot of weight, and her shrewish expression didn't help. "Let's try that new oyster bar near South Coast Plaza. All my friends rave about it, and you never take me anywhere."

Nora should have fled. Too late, she saw recognition

flash in Reese's blue eyes, which were as brilliant and hypnotic as ever. And, as always, his gaze swept her in instant assessment.

Was that rueful admiration she saw? She'd always felt at such a disadvantage, being older and plainer than Persia, that she enjoyed one-upping her former rival for a change.

Pathetic, Nora. Honestly, why should you care?

"How's it going?" she asked pleasantly.

"Well, look who's here." Persia raked her with a mixture of arrogance and apprehension. What did she think, that Nora would try to reclaim her unfaithful ex-husband?

"I happen to work here," Nora said.

"You're looking good. Very good." Reese sounded surprised.

Her ex-husband was as suave and men's-magazine-handsome as ever. Yet Nora no longer felt like an awkward teenager in his presence. There was something too calculated and overgroomed about him.

He certainly didn't compare to the rugged man she'd just noticed swinging out of the elevator. What had brought Leo here?

At the moment, Nora didn't care. His powerful presence eclipsed her ex-husband, and she really, really deserved a moment of payback.

"There you are!" she declared as if she'd been expecting him.

Leo barely broke stride. He took in the other couple, and she saw a flicker of understanding as he grasped the situation. Thank goodness practically everybody in Safe Harbor knew who Reese Kendall was.

Nora hoped Leo would play along. But considering the issues between them, how could she expect him to cooperate?

By doing so, he would also risk offending one of the town's power players. She was being unreasonable, Nora thought, and braced for Leo to coolly put her in her place.

Chapter Thirteen

To Leo, Reese Kendall appeared even slicker in person than in his pictures in the paper. So this was the jerk who'd tossed Nora aside for his barely-out-of-school wife. As for the new Mrs. Kendall, the chubbiness didn't detract from her exotic beauty nearly as much as that petulant expression.

He'd stopped by only to ask for a few minutes of Nora's time. No way was he going to let these snobs score a round at her expense, though.

"Hi." He slid an arm around her waist and nuzzled her temple. The scent of flowers and femininity tingled through his senses.

From the way she shifted against him, no one could miss the fact that they were lovers. "Leo, I don't know if you've met my ex-husband, Reese, and his wife, Persia."

Keeping his arm anchored around Nora, Leo shook the other man's hand. To Persia, he said, "Congratulations."

She glanced at her rounded midsection. "It's a girl. I'm due in August. The doctor says I'm extremely healthy, but I refuse to have natural childbirth. Why should women suffer? We don't live in the Stone Age."

She didn't appear to expect anything other than agreement, so Leo merely nodded.

"You're a friend of Nora's?" Reese asked, as if it weren't obvious.

"We hang out." Leo grinned to indicate this was an understatement. "Don't know how you let her get away, but hey, I'm glad you did."

Was he laying it on too thick? The gratitude in Nora's expression reassured him. He was sure going to miss being around her.

"We're off," she told her ex. "Nice to see you."

"Nice to see you, too." Was that regret tightening his mouth? Served the jerk right.

Persia tugged his arm. "Come on, Reese. I'm starving. Call the damn cook and tell her we're eating out."

"Have a good time." Leo let a hint of irony bleed through, and sliding his hand down to Nora's shapely rear end, he steered her along the hall.

"How was I?" he said after the elevator doors closed them inside.

"Brilliant." Nora brushed her cheek across his shoulder. "My best birthday present ever."

"It's your birthday?" He hated to spoil the occasion.

"I'm thirty-five." She nibbled on his earlobe. "Way older than you."

He was getting hot. Surely pregnancy didn't require complete abstinence, did it? "Guess that makes you a cougar."

"Grrr," she murmured close to his ear.

Leo's body went hard as iron. "If you don't have any plans for your birthday, we could have dinner. Or skip dinner and cut to dessert."

"That whole candles-on-the-cake business is overrated."

"I didn't mean that kind of dessert."

"Neither did I."

They probably broke the sound barrier en route to her condo. When they entered, Leo was in such a hurry he nailed Nora right on the living-room sofa. Not the casting couch—they didn't make it as far as the den.

"I guess that answers my question," he said afterward as they lay side by side, entwined and entangled.

"What question?" She wiggled, brushing his sensitive core, but he was spent. In an hour or so, he'd undoubtedly spring back to life.

Maybe sooner.

"About whether pregnant women are allowed to have sex," Leo said.

"Unless there are contraindications, sure."

He traced a hand lazily across her breasts. He'd been right—they *were* bigger. "And you don't have any of those?"

"No bleeding or preterm labor," Nora responded. "Later on, couples do have to get creative about positions."

"Creative is good."

"Creative is very good."

Hazily, Leo recalled that he'd only planned to meet with Nora to tell her they needed to put distance between them. That distance, at the moment, amounted to less than a centimeter.

He was grateful her ex-husband's presence had given him a reason to flirt with her. And to find out what a special occasion this was. "Happy birthday. Did I say that already?"

"Yes. Let me know when you're ready to celebrate again."

His motor was definitely revving. But pregnant women needed to eat. "You must be hungry."

She brushed back the hair tangling around her face and slender neck. "I have leftover pasta."

"Sounds good to me." He rose to his feet.

She held out a hand and let Leo pull her up. Her arms

slipped around him and they stood, holding each other, stark naked in her living room.

"We have to stop doing this," he told her. "It's muddling my brain."

"What's wrong with muddling?"

"Good point."

After eating, they headed for the shower and soaped each other thoroughly. Leo found himself sneaking glances at her stomach, wondering how long it took before you could see the baby growing.

What had Ralph said? *"When it comes out, it'll be a whole new person."* Strange how he was beginning to find that prospect fascinating. "You haven't told me when you're due."

"November," Nora said.

"Boy or girl?"

"Too soon to tell." She turned off the water and reached for a towel.

He wondered if there were some way to stay involved without…without what? *Without getting bogged down in expectations and obligations. Without quarreling, sniping, baiting each other or relaunching the Cold War.*

Leo knew that not all relationships deteriorated. But he had two strikes against him—being a cop, and having grown up in a home where the parents might as well have lived in different countries. Add Nora's failed marriage, and that made three strikes between the pair of them.

Anyway, he had no time for a serious relationship. After that scene with Captain Reed this morning, he'd better focus on his promotion or he'd be stuck on patrol for the rest of his life.

The hair dryer cut off. "You've run through enough expressions for an entire soap-opera season," Nora said. "Are you mad at me?"

"What makes you think that?" He pulled a comb through his damp hair.

"Let's start with the frown and move on to the scowling."

He hadn't meant to bring this up, but he might as well. "The captain called me into his office this morning. Violet informed her ex-boyfriend that I was investigating his family, and the Hightowers complained to the chief."

Her eyes widened. "I never meant to get you in trouble."

Leo felt a tug of remorse. "This isn't your fault. But if Violet's mom receives any more threats, she should make a formal report. I can't be involved."

Nora drew on a pair of jeans, tugging hard to get them fastened. "I don't want to involve you in anything else, either. Only, this odd thing happened today. It isn't illegal, or at least, I don't think so, but I could use your opinion."

Leaning in the doorway, Leo watched her fumble with the buttons on a blouse that refused to close. "You expect me to concentrate while you're sticking your breasts in my face?"

She stared down at the blouse. "Gee, there's one plus to getting knocked up. I got bigger."

Leo found her so cute, he had to restrain the impulse to undress her again. "If you're concerned about legalities, you should ask my brother. Tony's a lawyer, and he does work at your hospital."

She discarded the shirt and selected a jersey. "I hate to risk stirring up a hornet's nest over nothing. Also, I'm concerned about patient confidentiality."

"If patient privacy is an issue, you shouldn't tell me, either."

"I wasn't going to mention any *names*."

What if there genuinely was a public safety problem in Safe Harbor? Leo didn't kid himself that unearthing a scandal would score points for him; more likely, he'd be sticking his neck in a noose. All the same, he hated to ignore a potentially serious issue. "Go ahead. I'm listening."

She didn't get to respond, because her phone rang.

"You on call?" he asked.

"No." She checked the phone's display. "But it's the hospital. That's odd." Into the mobile, she said, "Dr. Kendall."

She listened intently for a moment, responded, "I'll be right there," and clicked off. "Suzy's been admitted and she wants me there. She may be having a miscarriage."

Leo pictured Ralph's broad face alight with eagerness as he'd talked about welcoming his child into the world. The kid had mapped out an entire future, and now it might be disappearing. "That's rotten luck. Ralph's likely to be in crisis."

"Want to come?" she asked. "I have a feeling he's going to need support."

"I'll drive."

She didn't argue.

On the way over, Nora told Leo about the two patients who'd been contacted by an adoption attorney. She half-expected him to dismiss the issue as irrelevant, but instead he drew out his pad at a stop sign and took a few notes.

"Did they mention the name of the attorney?" he asked.

She shook her head. "It didn't come up."

"Any chance you could find out?"

Nora supposed she could make some excuse to call and ask. "I'll try. Why?"

He steered into the hospital parking structure. "Eleanor Wycliff complained about someone leaving an adoption attorney's cards at the counseling center. It might be a link."

The possibility of a connection, however remote, troubled Nora. "Neither of my patients is a client at the center, as far as I know."

"But the center used to be headquartered at the hospital," Leo pointed out. "And there's a lot of connections through the volunteer staff."

"You think we should notify Samantha?" Nora asked.

"I have the impression she tends to go off half-cocked."

That was putting it mildly. "If she learned someone might be abusing her clinic, she'd have a conniption."

"Is that a medical term? Does it hurt?" Leo teased.

Nora laughed. "My grandmother used to say that. I think it's really ancient slang for a hissy fit. Or is that ancient slang, too?"

"I have no idea, but let's leave Dr. Forrest and her temper in the dark for now." He killed the engine. "After getting called on the carpet at work, I prefer to proceed with caution. Why don't you start by asking about the attorney? If your patients didn't use Fergus Bridger, there's nothing to investigate."

"That's his name?" Nora asked as they got out.

"The very man."

"I never heard of him."

"You have now."

As they hurried toward the hospital's labor-and-delivery unit, she stopped thinking about the attorney's possible shenanigans. There were more immediate issues to confront.

While Suzy might have intended to relinquish her baby, a miscarriage could hit a lot harder than anyone expected. No telling how she and Ralph might react.

Thank goodness Leo was here, Nora thought, and held his hand in the elevator.

THEY LEARNED WHEN THEY arrived that Suzy had lost the baby. Nora rushed to comfort the girl, who'd apparently declined to summon her family and was refusing to see Ralph, either.

Leo found the young man pacing across an otherwise empty patient lounge, his unshaven cheeks wet with tears. As part of his professional training, Leo had taken courses in consoling crime victims and offering support to fellow officers who'd suffered trauma. In his five years on the force in this quiet town, however, he'd rarely drawn on those skills. And nothing had prepared him to help a boy suffering such a devastating and unexpected loss.

"She won't even talk to me," Ralph muttered. "I was with her when she started cramping. Why won't she let me stay with her?"

As if Leo understood women! Then a possible explanation occurred to him. "Maybe she doesn't want to deal with your feelings. Are you angry?" Anger would be a natural reaction, since Ralph had wanted the baby so badly and Suzy hadn't.

"Yeah." Ralph nodded slowly. "Yeah, I guess I am."

"At Suzy?" Leo took a seat.

Ralph shoved his hands into his jeans pockets. "If she cared more, maybe the baby would have lived."

Leo doubted maternal hostility caused miscarriages or there'd be fewer unwanted babies. "I doubt her emotions have anything to do with it. Did the doctor say what went wrong?"

"He said they'd run some tests." The boy stopped pacing. "I can't believe this is happening. The baby seemed so real."

And mine feels so unreal.

The perception startled Leo. He didn't envision the

fetus inside Nora as a baby like Tara. But it was, or soon would be.

"You think Suzy picked up on what I was thinking?" Ralph asked. "Is that why she doesn't want me around?"

"I think that's highly likely."

"But I still love her," the boy said miserably.

"Unlike in the movies, love doesn't necessarily conquer all," Leo observed.

"You ever been in love?"

Leo struggled to sort out his thoughts. If he couldn't make sense of his own feelings, how on earth was he supposed to help Ralph? "I thought I was, a few times. It felt intense, and the breakups hurt like hell, but the relationships wouldn't have lasted."

"How can you be sure?"

Good question. "I missed the idea of the woman more than the actual person. It didn't take long for me to realize they could be replaced."

"I can't replace Suzy," Ralph said dejectedly. "We used to be best friends. We talked about everything. I never figured a girl as smart and pretty as her could care about me."

"Well, you haven't necessarily lost her. Just hang in there." That was the best Leo could come up with.

Footsteps approached. Even before he saw her, he knew it was Nora.

She blinked back the tears darkening her eyes. "How're you doing, Ralph?"

"Not so good."

She lowered herself carefully onto the edge of a couch, moving so stiffly that Leo wondered if she'd strained a muscle. "Do you have any questions?"

Ralph's mouth trembled, although whether in anger or grief, Leo couldn't tell. "Why did this happen? Is it because Suzy hates the baby?"

Nora wrapped her arms around herself. "She doesn't, Ralph. You should see how broken up she is. Motherhood is a complicated business. So is fatherhood, as I guess you know."

"If she loved it, she wouldn't have wanted to give it away," he said.

"That's not necessarily true. To her, giving a baby to the right parents seemed like an act of love. The miscarriage... She's devastated. She needs your support. But if you're going to blame her, it's better that you stay away."

He ducked his head. "I just wish I knew why this happened."

Leo wanted the answer to a different question—why Nora had been avoiding his gaze since she entered the lounge. Was she just empathizing with Suzy, or was she holding something back?

Whatever it was, she didn't intend to say it in front of Ralph. Instead, she straightened, shifting to full doctor mode. "Between 10 and 25 percent of all clinically recognized pregnancies—pregnancies doctors have confirmed—end in miscarriage. It's far more common than people realize."

"But why?" the boy pressed.

"We can't always find a cause." Strands of blond hair wisped around her face. "Often, something goes wrong very early, with the chromosomes or the cell division. That means the baby couldn't have survived."

He was crying openly. "He never had a chance?"

She handed him a tissue from a box set out on an end table and used another to dab her own eyes. "Probably not. Suzy didn't do anything wrong, and neither did you. It wasn't a matter of getting jostled or eating the wrong thing or thinking the wrong thoughts. The good news is that having a miscarriage doesn't usually preclude the mom from having future healthy children."

"As if she'd want to. With me, anyway." Ralph blew his nose.

"I suspect she might, when she's ready. Right now, she's worried that you'll never forgive her for losing the baby."

"She is?" Ralph swallowed visibly. "She'd like to see me?"

A tremulous smile warmed Nora's face. "She sent me out here to talk to you. She wants to see you, very much."

"All right!" He jumped up. "Thank you, Dr. Kendall." He pumped her arm and ran out of the lounge.

Nora, who'd risen gingerly, drew a deep breath. Instinctively, Leo moved to take her arm. "What's wrong?"

"Well…"

His gut tightened. There *was* a problem. "What, honey?"

She fixed her gaze in the vicinity of his shoulder. Why wouldn't she look at him?

"I…I'm afraid I might be having a miscarriage, too," she said.

Chapter Fourteen

Nora steeled her resolve. She wasn't going to melt down in front of Leo. And she certainly wasn't going to point out the irony that their situations were reversed from Ralph's and Suzy's.

This wasn't his fault, any more than Suzy was responsible for her miscarriage. Besides, Nora didn't feel any cramping.

Not yet.

"Shouldn't you be lying down?" Leo asked.

He sounded so worried that Nora's heart squeezed. "It's unlikely to make a difference. With a problem this early, there's no way to prevent it."

"You idiot," he muttered close to her ear. "I'm talking about how *you* feel. What kind of symptoms, I mean…what's going on?"

Alone with him in the lounge, she fought the impulse to nestle into the shelter of his arms. "I'm spotting. Bleeding a little."

"That sounds bad." He took her hand.

"There are several reasons why women might bleed early in pregnancy. Not all of them are serious." Since there was nothing to be done, she didn't want to dwell on this. "Come on. I want to be sure Suzy's all right."

Leo kept her hand enclosed in his. "You sure? You may

be a doctor, but that doesn't mean you're careful enough about your own health."

Although she appreciated his support, she removed her hand from his. They were about to step into a hallway, where they might run into any number of her coworkers. "I'm fine."

"We're surrounded by doctors. Let's have one of them check you out."

She'd already taken care of that. "I called my friend Paige. Dr. Paige Brennan. She's an ob-gyn in Newport Beach and I asked her to supervise my pregnancy. Her service promised to have her call me right back."

"There are doctors right here," he insisted.

"I'll wait." Nora respected the obstetrician attending Suzy, Dr. Zachary Sargent, an intense young ob-gyn who'd recently joined the staff. And her own pregnancy was hardly a state secret. But she felt an instinctive need to keep this deep hurt private. "Besides, with you hovering over me, everybody would figure out real quick who the father is. It's better if we do this somewhere else."

"We can worry about that later."

"Let's give Paige a few minutes to call me." She led the way down the hall, taking care to avoid jolting movements. Although she wasn't in pain, she felt fragile.

Leo kept close beside her, as if ready to swoop her up at the first sign of collapse. Despite her resolve not to read too much into this, Nora was grateful for his nearness.

They found Ralph and Suzy cuddled together on the bed, arms around each other and faces wet with tears. "I'm sorry I ignored how you felt," she was telling him. "This was your baby as much as mine. Don't be mad, okay?"

"I'm staying right here," he answered. "You're my girl. You always will be."

Nora strove for a professional air. "Everything all right?"

"We're okay," Suzy said.

"The important thing is, we're together," Ralph told her.

The tremulous smile on Suzy's face lifted Nora's spirits. The girl was going to recover. There'd be painful moments ahead and she'd never forget the baby she lost, but she didn't have to go into the future alone.

Abruptly, a wave of hot, raw envy washed over Nora. Unreasonable, unworthy, completely unprofessional envy. Yet with an ache that seemed to echo through her bones, she craved this kind of love in her life. To be truly and unreservedly cherished by a guy who put her before everything else. Who would stand by her, be her partner and lover, care for her no matter what happened. And cherish her children, too, not as an obligation but from an abundance of love. Although this young couple before her might not even be twenty years old, they'd found something she might never know.

Then her gaze fell on Leo. Standing right there, watching her, ready to take action if she needed him. Was it possible he might be changing?

"We can have more children," Ralph was saying. "You do want children someday, don't you?"

"Sure, in a few years." Suzy's forehead wrinkled. "I didn't choose to be pregnant, but I got used to the idea that I was sheltering a life. I started picturing this baby, even if I wasn't going to raise it myself."

"When you're ready, you'll make a wonderful mother."

Ralph's words painfully reminded Nora of her own threatened miscarriage. Anxious to check her symptoms, she could hardly bear to stay in the room a moment longer. But she had to make sure Suzy was all right.

"Do you want me to stay?" she asked the girl, and tried to ignore Leo's disbelieving look.

"No, thanks, Dr. Kendall. I'm okay."

"You have my number," Nora reminded her. "I hope I'll see you at the counseling center again. Saturday, if you're up to it." Even if she lost her own baby, Nora should be well enough by then.

"Thanks," the girl said. "I'd like that."

Finally, Nora escaped into the corridor. She felt as if she'd been holding her breath for hours.

Leo exited right behind her. "I'm not sure if you're a saint or a maniac," he said. "With what you're going through, you should be taking care of yourself first."

"I chose this profession because I love helping others," Nora replied. "It's a privilege. Don't you feel the same way about serving the public?"

"Not always," he admitted. "As a cop, you see the worst of human behavior. It's easy to get cynical. But being around Ralph reminds me why I chose this job."

Zack Sargent came around the corner, looking every inch the caring physician in his white coat. "Ask him to check you over," Leo murmured. "Please?"

Zack must have noticed them looking his way, because he paused. "Something I can do for you, Nora?"

"No, thanks." Her phone vibrated and she drew it quickly from her pocket. To her relief, the name on the screen read Paige Brennan. "As a matter of fact, everything's taken care of."

LEO WAS GLAD TO SEE THAT doctors, like cops, were willing to do favors for friends. Dr. Brennan could have referred Nora to whatever colleague was on call at the hospital where she practiced, but instead she met them at her office suite in Newport Beach. Located in a cluster of one-story buildings, the office had her name and those of three other doctors on the door.

The place was closed for the evening, but no matter. Off went the alarm, on went the lights and they were in business.

A tall woman with dramatic red hair and a lab coat thrown over her jeans and sweater, Dr. Brennan asked Nora a few questions and got her prepped in an examining room with a portable ultrasound machine. Positioned on a large, wheeled frame, the device resembled a computer, complete with screen and keyboard.

Nora lay on the examining table in a flimsy hospital gown that was open at the front. "Let's have a look and find out what's happening," Dr. Brennan said.

She didn't fuss or offer sympathy, for which Leo was grateful. On the drive over, he'd noticed Nora blinking back tears. Her whole body seemed tight, shoulders held tautly, fists clenched in her lap. Now, the doctor's calm professionalism seemed to soothe her, and it eased the situation for Leo, too.

Emotional drama had always been uncomfortable for him, and seeing Nora in distress alarmed him. Still, he couldn't have been anywhere else. He was partly responsible for putting her in this situation. And, even if they went their separate ways, he would always feel concerned for her well-being.

After spreading gel, Dr. Brennan moved a small scanning device over Nora's bare stomach. Black-and-white images shifted on the screen. How could the doctor tell anything from those curves and squiggly movements?

"If she's bleeding, shouldn't you do something about that first?" he asked, and wished he'd thought of this earlier. "I mean, like surgery or something?"

"She isn't bleeding heavily enough to be in any immediate

danger," the woman reassured him. "Let's see what's going on and then we can decide how to proceed."

He stifled the almost overwhelming urge to insist she take action. *Let the woman do her job.*

Each time the device stopped moving and the doctor peered intently at the screen, Leo nearly shouted with impatience. He wished he understood what it all meant. "What's it tell you?"

"Nothing yet. Ultrasound or sonography employs high-frequency sound waves. They bounce back and form a picture of the body's internal organs. It takes a while to get a firm idea of what's in there." Dr. Brennan's voice had an almost hypnotically calming effect. "This portable machine doesn't produce as dramatic images as some of the more advanced equipment, but we should be able to determine... Ah, there we are."

A tiny shape appeared on the screen. "It's still there?" Nora asked.

"Still there," Dr. Brennan confirmed. Pointing at the screen, she addressed them both. "You can see the head here, and the arm and leg buds. This is very early in gestation, but—there's the heart! Beating away. Incredible to think it might still be beating a century from now, isn't it?"

A chill ran through Leo. He was staring at the squiggly image of his own unborn baby. The beginnings of an individual who would grow up, perhaps marry, have children and become old.

It didn't seem possible.

The little creature shifted as if to protest the pressure from the device. "You aren't hurting him, are you? Or is it a her?"

"The reactions are perfectly normal. And it's too soon to tell the gender. Hold on." The doctor froze the frame and pressed a button. "I'll run off a copy for you. Baby's first photo." She smiled over at Nora. "I suppose you've done this a zillion times with your patients."

"This is different." Nora's eyes shone with wonder now, instead of tears. "You're sure everything's all right?"

"I don't see any problems, but let me check around."

"You mean, something could still be wrong?" Leo asked as the tiny figure on the screen continued to wriggle.

"Sometimes the placenta—the organ that nourishes the baby—attaches low in the uterus," Dr. Brennan told him. "That might cause bleeding. Nope, looks fine."

"*Something* caused it," he pointed out doggedly.

"It could be my cervix," Nora said, adding for his benefit, "That's the neck of the uterus."

"The cervix can be very tender and sensitive. In some women, it's easily irritated." Dr. Brennan clicked off the screen. "You didn't by any chance have intercourse earlier tonight, did you?"

Leo felt himself flush. "That could cause problems? I mean, I guessed that it might, but Nora said everything was okay."

"Might want to refrain for a while, Dad," the doctor said. "Sex isn't likely to cause a miscarriage but we don't like to see bleeding, so I recommend holding off."

"Not a problem." That wasn't entirely true. With Nora beaming, he felt a strong urge to pick her up and cuddle her, and he had a pretty damn good idea where that would lead. Man, this was going to be a long nine months. No, wait, about seven more months until November.

Seven months until he got to hold his kid. Until this little person peered up at him and made funny noises. Smells, too.

The doctor had called him Dad. Yep, Leo was going to be a father, like Tony. Even though he'd known about the pregnancy for a few days, it was still hard to wrap his mind around the notion.

Well, the baby definitely seemed real to him now.

As Leo listened to the doctor tell Nora to take it easy for a few days, he wondered how they were going to work this out. Right away, he'd planned to provide financial support, but now he wanted more. How much more, he wasn't sure.

At last, the doctor went out. Watching Nora put on her clothes for the second time that evening, Leo felt a surge of warmth. "That's my baby."

She glanced at him uncertainly. "Well, yes."

He inhaled the scents of antiseptic and medicine overlying Nora's sweetness. "This is incredible. We have a lot to discuss."

"Absolutely." She turned away to fiddle with her purse. Looking for a brush, or hiding her expression?

Whatever was running through her mind, he'd find out soon enough. Maybe by then he'd figure out what was running through his.

A SHORT WHILE AGO, NORA'S world had been falling apart. Now, pure happiness welled up. She recalled a saying one of her college roommates had stuck on the wall of their dorm room—Suppose you lost everything you had, and then you got it back again?

That little fellow—or girl— inside her was lively and healthy. Miraculous. And the amazement on Leo's face thrilled her almost as much. It was as if he'd bonded with the baby while seeing it in the ultrasound.

She might be kidding herself, but Nora didn't think so. It was too much to hope that he loved her, too, or was it? On her birthday, maybe her dreams really could come true. All of them.

When they were ready, she thanked Paige. "Be sure to send me a bill."

"Are you kidding?" Her friend gave her a hug. "This was fun. Besides, it's part of your obstetrical package, so I *am* getting paid."

"You don't give everyone special treatment. I'd rather not take advantage."

"Well, you never know when I might need a favor. Like, maybe a reference."

"You're thinking of leaving here?" Nora asked in surprise.

"Not in the near future," her friend assured her, "but perhaps eventually. I'll see you at your next appointment."

"Great."

Paige turned to Leo. As they shook hands, Nora noted that they were almost the same height. "Nice to meet you."

"I appreciate everything you've done for Nora," he responded, his voice rich with gratitude.

Paige gave Nora a wink, as if to say, Way to go, girl! You caught a winner.

Leo was definitely that.

Nora knew she'd better not wish for too much. But right now she couldn't help it.

Chapter Fifteen

Whatever Leo had intended to say on the drive back to her condo, Nora missed it. She fell asleep almost the moment she settled into his car.

Blame it on pregnancy hormones, a long day and roller-coaster emotions. In any event, she didn't awaken until he was angling her in the seat, preparing to lift her out. They'd reached her condo complex, she noticed vaguely, and he'd managed to find a rare unoccupied visitor parking space.

"Oh, Leo." She brushed her cheek against his arm. "It's been an incredible day."

"And it isn't over yet."

He was staying. A good sign. "I can walk, you know."

"Lean on me."

"Glad to."

She leaned on him all the way inside, where he insisted on taking her straight into the bedroom. That might have been fun, had they not both been aware that they couldn't make love.

Besides, it was Monday night, and tomorrow they had to work. Leo had mentioned once that his shift started at the inconvenient hour of 6:30 a.m., which didn't allow time for him to go home and change.

If he lived here, that wouldn't pose a problem.

"Sit." Leo pointed to the edge of the bed. "Tell me where you keep your nightgown."

"You're dressing me?" she asked, delighted.

He swept her with a wry look. "Undressing you. *And* dressing you for bed. You heard what the doctor said. You have to take it easy."

"The pink one, hanging on the peg." Much as she hated to call in sick tomorrow, Nora supposed she ought to. Perhaps Dr. Sargent, who hadn't yet established a full slate of patients, would be willing to help.

What luxury, to lie here while Leo waited on her. Through half-closed eyes, she enjoyed the lithe way he prowled through her closet, and the moment of clumsiness when he tried to lift her nightie so carefully that he lost his grip and sent it floating to the floor. "Oh, damn," he muttered.

"Butterfingers," she teased.

His expression of mingled amusement and annoyance set her to laughing. How comfortable it felt, having him here. How natural.

Where would they put the pool table? Well, they could work that out.

He captured the escaped nightie and brought it over. "Okay, now what should I do?"

He apparently hadn't considered that she was going to have to get up to brush her teeth, but never mind. "Sit here and talk to me," Nora said.

Leo edged onto the bed. "How're you feeling?"

"Euphoric," she admitted. "You were wonderful to-night."

His hands stroked along her arms. "So much has changed."

"Because you saw the baby?"

"I saw a lot of things." Deep breath. "Funny how I never

expected to learn from Ralph. I mean, he's just a kid. But he's a man, too."

The reminder of Suzy and Ralph's loss gave Nora a guilty twinge, as if she shouldn't be enjoying her good fortune quite so much. But what harm could it do? "They're growing up fast. Tell me what you learned."

"That I can't keep at arm's length from my child." Leo's voice had a rough edge. He was struggling with this, she realized. Why did it have to be so complicated? "My family didn't exactly give me a good example of how to relate to people."

"They can't have been too bad." Nora had seen the closeness between Leo and his brother.

He shrugged. "We weren't some soap opera, but we managed to be toxic in our own special way. My kid sister was an invalid who died when she was eleven, and Mom was so wrapped up in Tara, she hardly knew I existed. Dad only loved us when we won awards and got top grades. Tony excelled at that, but not me. I rebelled, and acted like a jerk most of the time. That's the short version."

From the way he ground out the words, Nora gathered the wounds had never fully healed. Instinctively, she yearned to soothe away the pain. But they were talking about their own baby, their own family, not the past.

"You don't have to live the way your parents did," she pointed out. "Look at your brother."

"That's what you expect from me?" His gaze was sharp. "The nine-to-five job, the house on the bluffs?"

Nora blinked in surprise. "I was talking about the way he and Kate work together. Raising their kids. Supporting each other."

"I'm not Tony. Never will be."

"That's not what I'm asking." She longed to brush the tension from his jaw. She wished she could restore the sweetness she'd seen in him earlier. "Forget I mentioned him. You said we had a lot to discuss."

Cool air replaced the warmth as Leo got to his feet. "I've been turning things over in my mind, trying to figure out how to get a handle on this. You and I—well, we both knew this was temporary, but suddenly it isn't. Because of the baby. On the other hand, I'm still the same person as always."

"Fundamentally, sure." The same person with as much capacity to love as his brother or anyone else. Nora hoped he could see that.

"I can deal with being an uncle. More than an uncle, I suppose, since there'd be financial support and more one-on-one time and all that. But I can be *like* an uncle." He took a firm stance, legs apart, as if bracing for attack. "The kid will have as much of a dad as a lot of children in divorce situations."

Divorce situations? An uncle? Pain twisted through Nora. "I thought you refused to hold your child at arm's length. I thought…" *You idiot. You thought he was falling in love with you.*

"That's not what I'm talking about. I'm proposing a reasonable compromise." In his gaze, she saw an odd mix of stubbornness and offended innocence.

Unexpectedly, she felt a burst of anger. Anger at him for ducking his feelings and retreating into his tough-guy protective shell. Anger at herself for falling in love with yet another man who couldn't love her back.

Unlike Reese, who was too self-absorbed to truly care for others, Leo had everything she'd dreamed of. He just wasn't willing to share it with her.

Tears burned her eyes, but Nora refused to yield. Unlike earlier this evening when she'd feared a miscarriage, she wasn't helpless. This time, she had a choice. "I'm not interested in my child having an uncle. If you can't be a father, then—well, I don't know what you are."

"That's unfair."

"Maybe to you. Not to me." She felt like jumping up and shaking him, and that scared her. She wasn't used to lashing out, didn't know the boundaries of her own rage. "You should leave."

"You won't even talk to me?" He remained planted by the door.

"What else is there to say? This isn't a discussion, it's a take-it-or-leave-it. Well, I refuse to raise a child around the edges of your life. I might find someone else who wants to be a husband and a full-time father, and if not, I'm better off alone." Nora bit back a flood of furious words, none of which would convey what she felt, anyway. Which was hurt. Just…hurt.

What he should have done was crossed the room and hugged her. What he did was draw back. "This is exactly what I mean. All this drama. I don't know what kind of man you're looking for, but it isn't me."

If only she had the power to rewind to an hour ago. To return to Paige's office, to that moment when happiness hovered within grasp. But even if she could, events would play out just as they had, because she was Nora and he was Leo. "I'm sorry you feel that way."

"Sleep on it." He spoke gruffly. "Maybe tomorrow…"

She refused to go through this wringer again so soon. "I need longer."

"How much longer?"

"I don't know."

"Fine." Coldness, with a side of sarcasm. "Call me when you're ready." Out he went.

An urge to yell after him seized Nora. *Don't go!* Except, if he turned around, she had no idea what she'd say.

She heard his footsteps as he crossed the living room and the sound of the front door closing. Then the knob jiggled as he made sure it was locked.

Taking care of her, even as he left.

That failed to soften her rage. For heaven's sake, he'd basically expected her to spend the next twenty years tied to him, with no real obligation on his part other than a financial one.

Nora tried to retreat into the idea that had comforted her, marginally, as she'd fought through her divorce. The belief that eventually she *would* find the right guy. That there had to be a man out there worthy of her love and ready to love her back.

But she wasn't going to fall for some other man. She'd fallen too hard for Leo.

The only solution was to give him up entirely. Later, they could deal with the whole legal parenthood issue, but for now, she had to protect her heart.

HALF A DOZEN TIMES THAT week, Leo nearly pressed Nora's number on his phone. But he'd gone that route after their initial encounter, and she'd cut him off. This time, let her make the first move.

He'd proposed a perfectly reasonable compromise. One way or another, he planned to remain involved with his child. As involved as he could be.

Living alone suited Leo. He liked grabbing leftover pizza out of the refrigerator and eating over the sink. In the middle of the night, when he awoke feeling irritable, he enjoyed knocking billiard balls around with satisfying thunks, and no worries about disturbing a wife or roommate.

He wasn't fond of the discolored paint at the front of the house, though. On his day off, he slogged to the paint store to match the color of the shutters, prepped the surface and touched them up. He also mixed some concrete and filled the crack in the porch. When his neighbor's gardener, noticing the improvement, proposed to weed and reseed the lawn, Leo forked over the cash.

Wouldn't want his kid to grow up thinking Daddy lived in a dump.

The atmosphere at work didn't exactly thrill him, either. Trent Horner's self-satisfied grin proved a constant reminder that the two-week evaluation period was drawing to a close. Trent had progressed from running errands for the sergeant to cozying up to Chief Walters. With the public information officer out on maternity leave, there always seemed to be some community group touring the department or school requesting a friendly officer for career day. And Trent popped up like a plastic figure in an arcade game of Whac-A-Mole.

"Everybody knows he's nothing but a suck-up. The captain sees right through him," Patty commented on Saturday as Leo steered the cruiser past a park. On a mild April afternoon, it teemed with families and kids.

"Maybe so, but it bothers me. The brass shouldn't be handling promotions in such a subjective manner." Most police departments at least gave the appearance of objectivity in the way they tested, interviewed and scored candidates, although Leo suspected there was plenty of behind-the-scenes bias at work. "One day some disgruntled candidate's going to sue them."

"Safe Harbor's a small town," Patty pointed out. "They do a lot of things the old-fashioned way."

Leo shrugged. "Not that it matters. As far as I'm concerned, you've earned the promotion. Congratulations."

He meant it, more or less. She'd focused hard on working with Mike, while Leo hadn't done much of anything except get distracted by his love life. Sure, he'd investigated his cases thoroughly and gone into careful detail in his reports, but that episode with the Hightowers and the chief had put him in a bad light.

"Mike's a good teacher," his partner said. "Goes out of his way to clue me in. I'm not sure why."

"Maybe he likes you." Leo scanned a parked car that resembled one sought in a bank robbery in Huntington Beach. Right make and model. Green instead of blue, though.

"You mean, personally?"

"Naw, I bet he likes you impersonally."

"Funny thing is, he keeps asking about my long-term plans. Where do I see myself in ten years, ever get tired of the bureaucracy, that kind of thing." She drummed a rhythm on the dashboard.

"He's suggesting you join his agency?" Leo hadn't realized Mike was seeking anyone else to work with him and his partner. "He must be nuts."

"Why?"

"You, strike out on your own? No regular paycheck, no pension? It's not your style." He studied a man sitting on a park bench. Suspicious, a lone guy in a park full of children, but the fellow appeared absorbed in his newspaper. Plus he'd chosen a seat facing away from the playground.

"I don't want to turn into some fat, middle-aged bureaucrat," she retorted. "Because that's what can happen in this job if you don't look out for yourself."

She had a point. If Leo lost the promotion, perhaps he should consider joining the agency himself.

No way. In spite of the frustrations that came with being a cop, he enjoyed the camaraderie of the force and the sense of making a difference in the community. Guess he wasn't such a rebel, after all.

"Sounds like you're considering his offer," he said, and signaled a turn.

"Nothing to consider," she shot back. "He hasn't offered. Hey, no circling back."

"Why not?"

"We've been sticking to this side of town since lunch."

"It isn't intentional." Their patrols deliberately resisted any predictable pattern.

"You're avoiding the Civic Center," Patty observed. "You and Blondie on the outs?"

Leo gritted his teeth. Usually, he appreciated her bluntness. Today, it grated. "Going our separate ways. As you'd expect, knowing me."

"She seemed different from your other girlfriends."

"Different how?"

"She's got guts," Patty said.

To prove he had nothing to hide, Leo swung in the opposite direction, toward the community center. "Since you're so crazy about her, let's see what she's up to."

"She's counseling today?"

He shrugged. To admit he knew about her plans with Suzy meant explaining the events of Monday night, which were none of Patty's concern. Besides, Leo didn't really expect to see Nora except from a distance.

Just enough to remind her that he existed. And that they had unfinished business.

Chapter Sixteen

Nora took Tuesday off work, but spent most of her time reviewing charts in the computer and consulting by phone. On Wednesday, glad to have no further spotting, she returned to the office.

Still, although she was at work, she didn't feel back to normal. Being pregnant changed everything. So did loving Leo, and missing him. Well, she would adjust—if only to the fact that becoming a single parent meant she had to keep right on adjusting.

To her relief, the office gossip had moved on to the subject of Bailey's surrogacy. The nurse announced that she'd come through her workup with flying colors and planned to start inseminations next month. Her sister, she reported, was already decorating the nursery.

Risking disappointment, but why not? Life didn't come with guarantees. Nora figured they should all enjoy the moment.

To pass her time, after work she got started on transforming her condo from a bachelorette pad into a real home. Buoyed by the ultrasound photo, she bought a teddy-bear mobile to put in the spare bedroom for baby Muffin—its temporary name, until she learned the gender—along with a portable crib to use on the patio while Nora leafed through medical journals, or in the kitchen while she cooked. She wanted to mull over the nursery decor a little longer before buying any more furniture.

As for calling Leo, she postponed that touchy topic to focus on the other phone calls she needed to make, to her patients who'd decided to adopt. The first woman she reached, Lucy Arrigo, happily informed her that attorney Fergus Bridger had produced a newborn much sooner than they'd expected.

Her voice shimmered with excitement. "We did pay him a lot, but it's worth it. Oh, he's so cute! Not Mr. Bridger—the baby. We're naming him Hernando, after my dad. My family's throwing us a huge party next weekend!"

Fergus Bridger. That was the lawyer Leo had mentioned. Still, in a small town, it wasn't unusual for a particular adoption attorney's name to turn up more than once. "Congratulations," Nora said. "If you don't mind my asking, how exactly did you find Mr. Bridger?"

"We got a call from a lady on his staff," Lucy replied. "She said someone had referred them to us. Whoever it was, they did us a huge favor."

"Did you sign up on a fertility website?"

"It's possible. Although I doubt I'd have put down my phone number."

No sense interrogating her further. This was a happy ending, after all. "I'm glad everything worked out."

On Friday, Nora got a call back from Una, who confirmed that her attorney was Fergus Bridger, too. Another mysterious, unspecified referral.

The patients seemed pleased, but if someone was leaking private information, Nora ought to tell the administrator and the hospital's attorney. It didn't feel right to share this with Tony, though, until she'd informed Leo.

Which meant she'd have to see him, or at least talk to him.

On Saturday, she met with both Suzy and Ralph at the picnic table outside the community center, since another counselor was seeing a client indoors. The young couple seemed sad, but resigned to their loss. They were working through the grief together, encouraging each other and facing the future with slowly building optimism.

"I'm sorry we lost our baby," Ralph confided, "but I can kind of see Suzy's point about how hard it would be right now. Becoming parents and all that."

His girlfriend nudged him. "Like we discussed, you can take business courses even if you aren't ready to pursue a degree."

"Yeah, I've been thinking about that," the young man conceded.

A question occurred to Nora. Reluctant as she was to poke into a sensitive issue, she had to bring it up. "Suzy, you said you found an adoption attorney here in Safe Harbor. Mind telling me who it was?"

"Mr. Bridger."

This had to be more than a coincidence. "Where'd you find his name?"

The girl's forehead creased. "Umm…I got a call from his office. They said someone referred me. It wasn't you, was it?"

"I would never give out your name or other information," Nora assured her.

"Anyway, he can go stuff his referral," Ralph said passionately.

Suzy chuckled, and the moment passed.

Nora had hoped Leo might stop by to see Ralph, but he hadn't arrived by the time the couple left. Inside the counseling center, she found May Chong straightening the array of brochures about family and medical services.

"Oh, you're finished," the secretary said.

"I hope you didn't stay on my behalf." The center's new security policies required at least two staffers to be on the premises at all times.

"No, no." May indicated the closed door to the inner room, from which came the faint murmur of voices. "We're busy today. I've been updating the schedule."

"Is Ted here? I need to buy a new printer and I'd appreciate his opinion." Realizing she might be taking advantage of the young man's good nature, Nora added, "I'll pay for his time as a consultant. I realize he has a business to run."

May's nose wrinkled. "Ha! He doesn't do much with that. Too busy on the internet."

Nora didn't understand. "Doing what on the internet?"

"Buying and selling things. And—" she lowered her voice "—gambling. I wish he'd quit. He says it's a hobby, but he loses money."

"You mean, a lot of money?" Nora didn't see how he could afford it.

The secretary's shoulders slumped. "He won't tell me exactly. But I think so."

Nora caught her breath at the implication. If Ted was addicted to gambling, he might have leaped at the chance to earn referral fees from the attorney. He had access to the computers. He also interacted with the girls who came here seeking help. That could explain how Bridger seemed able to come up with so many young moms.

Don't go off making half-cocked accusations. If she was wrong, she could hurt innocent people. Besides, now that Nora thought about it, Ted only worked on the counseling center's computers. They didn't contain her patients' records, and as far as she knew, neither Una nor Lucy was a client here.

The whole thing might be a coincidence. But she didn't really believe that.

Troubled, Nora picked up her purse, said goodbye to May and went out. She was nearing her car when she spotted the police cruiser with Leo at the wheel.

The sudden brightness in his expression when he glimpsed her mirrored her own rush of relief. They had to talk. She could trust Leo.

LEO WONDERED IF HE'D EVER be prepared for the sheer visceral impact of seeing Nora, her face glowing in the sunshine, her full lips parting as she waved at him. It took all his control to slow the car gradually and ease to one side instead of hitting the brakes.

"You're totally going your separate ways," Patty murmured. "You're totally not gawking at her like a smitten teenager and she's totally not hopping up and down in the parking lot. Hmm. Reminds me of high school."

"You drove around in a cop car in high school?"

"I drove around with guys who gawked at pretty girls," Patty grumbled. "That's why I took up target practice."

Leo double-parked—it saved time if they needed to pull away in a hurry—and got out. From long practice, he surveyed the area for anything amiss, which saved him from pulling Nora into his arms like an idiot.

All the same, as she drew near, he registered her vibrant restlessness and the rise and fall of her chest. "Anything wrong?" he asked.

"Can we talk?" In the bright light, her eyes took on an emerald brilliance.

"I'm on duty."

She gave him an exasperated look. "Not about us. About the adoption attorney."

Way to go, Leo. "Oh. Right." He signaled to Patty, who kicked open her door and came ambling over. "Dr. Kendall has some information for me. Mind taking a swing around the premises?"

Knowing grin. "Sure thing." She strolled to the car, informed the dispatcher of their location and walked away.

Nora watched Patty go. "She thinks this is personal."

"She *did* see you at my house. You left an impression."

"Somehow I never figured cops would gossip," Nora admitted.

"We're the worst." Leo leaned against the patrol car. Around them, he took in the usual comings and goings at the community center. A senior citizen in a colorful hat pushed her walker toward a car in a handicapped spot. Two women in jogging suits headed for the main building, perhaps to take an exercise class.

"I found out Ted Chong, our computer whiz, has no job and an internet gambling problem," Nora said in a rush. "His mom told me."

That got Leo's full attention. So did the information that Nora's patients had both received unexpected calls from Fergus Bridger's office.

"The thing is, neither Una nor Lucy comes here, so I don't see how he could access their information," she said. "He might be leaving the attorney's cards, but that's no big deal. And maybe he's given Bridger's name to some of the pregnant girls but… No, wait. Suzy received a call from the attorney's office. Another so-called referral."

"For a sizeable kickback if she used his services, no doubt." Leo folded his arms and considered how much, and how little, they'd uncovered. Stealing patient information was illegal, but as Nora had pointed out, her patients weren't in the counseling center computers, so there was no demonstrable link to Ted Chong. As for the attorney, Leo could imagine what a stink the guy would raise if they sullied his name without cold, hard proof. After the incident with the

Hightowers, he meant to be very, very careful. "Couldn't Mrs. Chong obtain the information at the hospital?"

Nora's hand flew to her mouth. "Yes, but I can't imagine she's involved."

"All the same, the hospital should hire an outside computer forensic specialist to check their system for breaches," he told her. "Does either of your patients wish to file a complaint against Fergus Bridger?"

To his surprise, Nora chuckled. "Quite the opposite. They're very pleased with his services. And to be honest, this takes me off the hook with the incoming head of our fertility program. He's been pressuring me to push them into aggressive treatment that they don't want. Now that they're adopting, it's a moot point."

While there may have been no harm done, the possibility of stolen information bothered Leo. Identity theft was a major problem, and he couldn't assume that someone with a gambling addiction would limit his misconduct. "I'll have to at least let my superiors know there's a possible issue here."

"Is that necessary? I thought this was confidential."

As they talked, he'd been keeping tabs on the dispatcher's chatter crackling from the cruiser radio. Now he caught a call for service. "Excuse me."

When Leo checked in, he learned there was a disturbance at an address he recognized. Rose's Posies.

The ramifications of this case were spreading already.

BIG CITIES HAD BIG CRIMES and horrific gut-wrenching scenes. Small towns occasionally suffered major crimes, too, and a fair sprinkling of minor ones. They also had annoying run-ins that big-city cops would dismiss without a backward glance.

Unfortunately, Leo couldn't afford to do that, especially

when the people in a dispute included City Councilman Roy Hightower.

The tiny flower shop was crammed with angry people as Leo and Patty approached. Through the glass front, he recognized Rose Nguyen, her face suffused with outrage; Violet, her large belly shaking as she reamed out a young man whose cheeks bore traces of acne, and a scowling Councilman Hightower. The man's heavy jowls got even heavier and jowlier when he spotted Leo.

"I don't think he likes me," Leo told Patty.

"Got it," she said, and moved forward to enter first. The tinkling of door chimes sounded absurdly pretty. "Someone call for assistance?"

"I did," Hightower and Rose Nguyen said simultaneously.

They'd both phoned. No wonder dispatch had put out a call for what appeared to be nothing more than a squabble.

The councilman addressed Patty. "Officer, your partner has a conflict of interest. He's taken it on himself to investigate my family, when we've done nothing wrong."

Patty cocked an eyebrow at Leo. He dredged up some hard-won patience. "Mr. Hightower, I assure you, I've done nothing of the sort. However, if you'd like us to summon another officer…"

"He isn't investigating you," Violet put in. "I just said that so Gary would stop hassling my mom."

"Officer Franco isn't targeting us?" the councilman said.

The girl shook her head. Leo felt like thanking her, except for the fact that she'd created this confusion in the first place. "I presumed the chief had cleared that up for you," he said.

"I wasn't sure whether to believe him," Hightower responded.

Leo addressed the others. "What can we do for you folks?"

Rose glowered at Gary Hightower. "He came in here and disrupted my store. Saturday's our busiest day." As if to underscore her point, a phone rang. "Mr. Tran!" she yelled.

The wizened man Leo had seen on their previous visit poked his head out of the back room. "Yes, yes." He disappeared, and the ringing stopped.

"I'm not the one causing trouble," Gary whined. "I'm here to clear things up. I'm sorry Violet got herself pregnant, but whoever's messing with her email, it's not me."

Rose Nguyen buzzed like an angry hornet. "Got herself pregnant? Like some magic trick?"

"I gave you my password!" the girl flared at her ex-boyfriend. "You're the only one who could have gotten into my email!"

"You're just trying to pressure me into paying you off!" To Patty, Gary said, "She called and screamed at me on the phone, so Dad and I drove over here. Well, look at her. She's still screaming."

"Am not!" the girl squealed.

Patty raised her hands, calling for calm. "What exactly do you believe this man has done, miss? And I'll need your names, please." She took out her pad and began jotting data.

Everyone calmed down at this indication that they were being taken seriously, and the story emerged with only occasional barbs flung between Violet and Gary. Under other circumstances, Leo and Patty would have separated the pair for questioning, but that seemed unnecessary.

Someone, both parties conceded, had used Violet's email account to send nasty messages to everyone in her address book, calling her ugly names and implying she was only interested in keeping her baby so she could extort money from the Hightowers.

Violet showed them an example on her smart phone that a friend had forwarded: "Tell her to quit being a b—and give the baby to parents who can take good care of it."

"I agree with the message, but I didn't send it," Gary concluded.

"Liar!" Violet flung at him.

"Let me see that." The elder Hightower took the phone and read through the message. "She sent this herself to get my son in trouble."

Violet glared at him. "That's a stupid idea."

"Or maybe your mother sent it."

"Don't be ridiculous!" Rose snapped.

Patty tapped her pen against the pad. "What makes you suggest that, Mr. Hightower?"

"From what Gary's told me, she doesn't want her daughter to keep the baby any more than we do," the councilman said. "Look at the end of the email, below the signature. There's an ad for an adoption attorney. I'll bet she cooked the whole thing up to add pressure."

An adoption attorney. Why was Leo not surprised?

Before he could speak, however, Violet faced her mother with a stricken expression. "Mom? The other emails, the ones with the threats—you said you deleted them. I never even saw them. *Did* you cook this up?"

The florist recoiled in shock. "No! Of course not!"

"But you don't want your grandchild. So you *could* have done it." Pain choked Violet's voice.

"I just hate to see you throw your life away." Her mother reached out gently. "I'm not sneaky. This sort of thing, I would never do."

Roy Hightower folded his arms, as if to say, *Case closed*.

But it wasn't. "I need to see that," Leo said, and took the phone.

There it was, below the email. An ad for Fergus Bridger.

Everything connected—Nora's patients, the business cards left at the center, the girls being referred to Bridger. Now all he and Patty had to do was figure out who was behind it.

Chapter Seventeen

Not until after Leo drove away from the community center did Nora realize the mistake she'd made. She'd mentioned her patients by name, or at least by their first names. Although she considered the conversation private, she shouldn't have violated their privacy.

Surely Leo wouldn't repeat that information to anyone or try to find out their full names, she reflected as she sat in her car, trying to figure out what to do next. Adding to her agitation was the address she'd heard over the police radio. She'd recognized it as Rose's flower shop. Leo had mentioned a disturbance, but what did that mean? A disgruntled customer, a shoplifter, a squabble between Violet and her mother?

Nora didn't want to intrude into police business, but she *was* Violet's counselor. Besides, the girl was eight months' pregnant. If she got upset, her blood pressure could skyrocket. Someone ought to keep an eye on things.

Someone like me.

Okay, it was a weak excuse for poking her nose where it didn't belong. All the same, Nora put the car into gear and drove the short distance, trying to figure out what she'd say when she got there.

And how she was going to impress upon Leo that he

couldn't, under any circumstances, try to contact her patients.

In front of the shop, she spotted the police cruiser. Through the window, she glimpsed the imposing figure of Councilman Hightower, whom she'd met several times when she was married to Reese. If the Hightowers were involved, this must be serious.

In the tiny rear lot, she squeezed the car into a space and got out. Immediately, her stomach churned a reminder that she'd missed her usual afternoon snack of crackers. Nora stopped, debating whether to retreat.

"You okay, lady?" A small Asian man appeared in the open back door of Rose's Posies. She'd seen him loading flowers in a truck on her last visit, she recalled.

"I'm—yes." She waved a hand apologetically.

"I saw you before, with Violet," he said. "You come in this way."

"Thank you." The prospect of cool air drew Nora forward. To her relief, the clean, natural scent of flowers banished the nausea as soon as she stepped inside.

From the front, she could hear raised voices. Back here, everything seemed peaceful. On a large table, a bouquet of lilies and other spring flowers, clearly a work in progress, was taking shape in a glass vase. She noticed what appeared to be a work order displayed on a computer screen. "Please don't let me stop you," she told the man.

"No problem." With a smile, he retrieved more blooms from a refrigerated case and resumed work.

The voices from the front rose and fell. Nora hovered out of sight, wondering if she should simply leave and call Leo later. The edge in Violet's voice stopped her, though, and soon Nora got caught up listening to angry cross-accusations.

Then she caught the name Fergus Bridger, spoken in

Leo's deep tones. Her knees suddenly weak, Nora gripped the edge of a counter. So the attorney was involved. Everything was connected somehow.

There'd been threats against Mrs. Nguyen, she recalled. Leo could hardly avoid filing an official report now. Did that have to include her patients' names?

"Violet, have you contacted this attorney?" Leo asked. "Did you give him any information about you?"

"Absolutely not!" came the girl's reply.

"You're sure you never called or emailed his office?"

"No."

They went on talking about whether anyone had borrowed her phone, or whether she'd sent emails from anyone else's computer. The answers were all negative.

Nora thought of Ted Chong. If he was relying on the referrals to help pay his gambling debts, Suzy's miscarriage must have cost him a hoped-for fee. Was it possible he'd stepped up the pressure out of desperation?

She'd introduced Ted to Violet. If he'd misused that acquaintance, she felt responsible.

Taking another deep breath, she stepped forward to make her presence known.

LEO HADN'T EXPECTED NORA to pop out of the back room. She was looking a bit pale, but determined. "Sorry to intrude, but I couldn't help overhearing," she said. "Mrs. Nguyen, has anyone worked on your computer recently?"

"Here at the store?" Rose frowned. "We were having some trouble. Violet called a repairman."

"Ted Chong, that guy from the counseling center," the girl said.

If Nora got any greener, somebody might mistake her for one of the plants, Leo thought, and guided her quickly to a chair. "Are you okay?"

Patty regarded them both curiously. Well, Leo would talk to her later.

"I'm fine," Nora said tightly. "Violet, did you give Ted your password?"

A pause. "Not exactly, but I keep all my passwords in a file. It's kind of hidden."

"You shouldn't keep anything like passwords or financial data on your hard drive," Leo told her.

"You think a computer repairman sent those emails?" Gary asked. "Man, that's weird."

"He volunteers at the counseling center," Violet said. "He seemed so friendly. Why would he do something like this?"

"We don't know that he did anything," Leo told her. "For now, Patty and I need to get everyone's contact information, and we'll look into this further."

Rose was outraged. "He was in my computer! You think he stole financial data?"

"You should change all your passwords and check with your bank to be sure there's no suspicious activity," Leo told her. "Also, place a fraud alert on your credit files. That way, creditors will contact you before they open any new accounts in your name."

She rushed into the rear of the store, no doubt to do exactly that. Violet followed.

"I hope the chief didn't come down on you too hard," Roy Hightower told Leo. "Looks like you were an innocent bystander. This girl told me lies. You can see why I wish my son had never met her."

Fire sparked in Nora's eyes. "She may get carried away, but she's planning to love and nurture your grandchild. You should admire her for that."

"I don't know what concern this is of yours, Mrs. Kendall," the councilman said tightly.

"It's *Doctor* Kendall," she answered tersely, standing to face him. "And it's my concern because I'm her friend."

"If you're her friend, talk her into putting the baby up for adoption. Then we can all get on with our lives." He turned to his son. "Come on, Gary. We're done here."

His son hesitated, and for the first time, Leo got the impression the boy might not be completely in agreement with his father. But he acquiesced without argument.

As soon as the pair disappeared out the door, Patty said, "Someone care to fill me in?"

Leo sketched the situation for her: the business cards at the counseling center, the threats to Rose's reputation, Ted's gambling problem, his mother's position at the hospital and the phone calls to Nora's patients. "No one filed any complaints and, until today, we didn't put the pieces together."

"Looks like we've got ourselves a case," she told him with a grin.

"Actually, you've got yourself a case." Much as he hated to yield control, he had to use good judgment. "You'd better write the report. If I were called as a witness in court, I'd have a conflict of interest." Partly because of his relationship with Nora, and also as a counselor at the center, he reflected.

Leo felt Nora's hand on his arm. "May I talk to you privately?" she asked.

"Of course."

"I'll go see if I can scare up an address for this Ted Chong." Patty sauntered out to the cruiser.

He and Nora were alone, surrounded by flowers and plants, wedding-themed decorations and lacy cards. Silly stuff, to Leo. What mattered was Nora's health. "You seem shaky. Maybe you should see that doctor again."

"I'm fine." She held on to him all the same.

He felt a powerful urge to take care of her. "You were turning green."

"It's only morning sickness," she told him firmly. "Leo, I had no right to mention my patients' names. You can't use them in your report. It's a violation of their confidentiality."

He hadn't given any thought to how he would handle that. "I don't even have their last names."

"And you can't try to find them out, either. I only mentioned them because I felt safe with you, Leo."

"And because you wanted to know if someone like Fergus Bridger had invaded their privacy."

"Of course! I have a responsibility to my patients."

He had a responsibility to protect other patients from identity thieves, but Leo refrained from mentioning that. Now that this was turning into a real case, he needed to stop discussing it with Nora.

As he'd pointed out earlier, either or both of them could end up getting grilled on a witness stand. Matters that seemed insignificant or merely personal looked very different when placed under a legal microscope.

The door tinkled open, admitting a young couple. From the back of the store, Violet hurried out to wait on them.

Time to go. "We'll have to notify the hospital administration," Leo told Nora as he held the door for her.

She didn't budge. "I'd rather call Dr. Rayburn myself."

"You should leave that to the police."

She lifted her hand from his arm. "I have to handle this my own way, Leo."

Nothing he could do to stop her. It was a free country. "I'll see you later."

"Yes."

He restrained a very unprofessional urge to kiss her sweet, upturned face, and to run his hand over her stomach, in which his tiny son or daughter nested snugly. But he was in uniform, and they were in public.

Instead, he went out to the cruiser, where Patty was tapping her fingers impatiently on the dashboard. "Got his address," she said as Leo slid in, and off they went.

A STUNNING ARRANGEMENT OF purple irises and pink tulips in a white vase soothed Nora, even though she couldn't smell them through the glass case. She simply had to take them home.

The price listed on the tag was well worth it. And since being around flowers seemed to ease her stomach, she could justify the indulgence for medical reasons.

Okay, that was stretching it. But so what?

"I can't charge you full price for this, Dr. Kendall," Violet said as Nora placed the bouquet on the counter. At the table, a young couple was busy paging through books of wedding arrangements.

"I insist on it," Nora told her. "How're you feeling? Any dizziness or pains?"

The girl accepted her money and rang up the sale. "I'm fine. I can't believe Ted would rip us off. He seemed so nice."

Nora couldn't believe it, either. "Did he actually steal from you?"

Violet shrugged. "My mom says her bank doesn't report any unusual activity. But trying to pressure me to give up my baby so he could make a commission—that's awful!"

Nora thought about her patients. True, they'd had a happy outcome by finding babies to adopt, but that didn't excuse someone's stealing their information. "How's your mother taking it?"

With a wry grin, Violet handed her the change. "All that stuff about grandchildren is starting to get to her. I heard her and Mr. Tran talking in Vietnamese about how precious babies are. He has something like five kids and ten grandkids, and my mom, well, she just has me."

"You think she might change her mind?" It would be wonderful if Rose helped her daughter raise the baby.

"Never can tell." There was a definite twinkle in Violet's eyes.

What a relief from the tension Nora had seen in her previously. And how ironic that Ted's machinations might have brought about this reconciliation.

Served him right that he wasn't going to earn a commission.

Nora shepherded her bouquet to her car, wedging it carefully onto the floor to avoid damaging the gorgeous blooms. In her condo, she cleared away a couple of books and set it on the coffee table, where she could enjoy it from all angles.

Then she put in a call she wasn't eager to make.

Mark Rayburn, who stayed available by cell even on the weekends, listened soberly to her account of her patients' unauthorized referrals to an adoption attorney and the suspicions about Ted Chong and his gambling problem. Apparently the officers hadn't had a chance to contact him yet, she gathered, and passed along Leo's recommendation about arranging a forensic audit.

"I can't believe May would be involved," Nora told him as she finished. "But someone apparently accessed their information, and I thought you should know."

"I'm glad you called," Mark said. "We take patient confidentiality and the security of our computer system very seriously. While these two couples are your private patients, they've also been seen at the hospital, haven't they?"

"That's right." Like other doctors at the medical office building, Nora had hospital privileges and used labs and a pharmacy owned by Safe Harbor Medical Center. Plus her computerized records were accessible to the hospital staff in case of emergency.

"I'll be happy to cooperate with the police when they call," he said. "And we will conduct that audit. As for May, I'll talk to her on Monday. I hope this is all a coincidence, but we'll have to see."

"I can't imagine an attorney stooping to stealing information," Nora said. "I mean, he could be disbarred."

"He might simply pay referral fees and turn a blind eye to where the information comes from," the administrator said. "He's probably cultivated sources all over town. I heard that local private adoptions took a hit thanks to all that publicity about surrendered babies. It inspired a lot of birth mothers to relinquish custody through the hospital." Some of the surrendered infants had been adopted by staff members, while most had been placed in loving homes through the county's social services agency.

Mark also promised to pass the information about Ted's behavior to his wife. Dr. Forrest would make sure the counseling center changed its passwords and barred the young man from the premises, he assured her.

The administrator didn't seem overly concerned about Nora's admission that she'd carelessly revealed her patients' first names to Leo. "This isn't a murder case. I doubt the police will expend the effort to call women all over town trying to figure out if someone made them happy against their will."

As she said goodbye, Nora hoped he was right. But Leo had a promotion at stake, and he'd never made any bones about what mattered to him.

Later that evening, when the doorbell rang and she saw

Leo's face through the peephole, Nora's chest constricted. Had he come to give her bad news?

And if he had, what was she going to do about it?

Chapter Eighteen

Nora had grown up feeling uncomfortable around men, tongue-tied and unprepared to handle their assumptions about how sexy and confident she was. Even after she married, she'd always feared that she was coming up short in Reese's eyes. When he announced that he'd found his soul mate—what an irony, in view of the scene she'd witnessed between him and Persia—it had seemed to confirm Nora's insecurities.

That made it even harder to explain why she didn't have those feelings around Leo. Never had, and didn't now. She just opened the door and they walked into each other's arms. Never mind the tensions between them. Forget about trust issues. They drew together like a pair of ice-skaters swooping into a spin, entwining without the least awkwardness.

"Missed you," he said as he kicked the door shut behind him.

"It's been practically a week." She didn't count their conversations today. Those had been impersonal.

His arms fit naturally around her as he drew her onto the couch and his lap. She burrowed into him, touching his jaw, tasting his mouth, nuzzling his hair.

"How's my baby?" he murmured into her hair.

"Much better. Morning sickness passed hours ago." Then,

seeing his gaze fix on her abdomen, she realized what he meant. "Oh, *this* baby."

"Both babies," he said, laughing.

"Well, I answered for the first one already. As for Muffin, he's still too small for me to feel him or her wiggling."

Leo settled back, holding her in place. "What kind of name is Muffin?"

"Temporary," Nora assured him.

"Our baby deserves a real name." Leo rubbed her shoulder lightly. "I'm thinking Leona if it's a girl and Leo Junior if it's a boy."

"Noreen and Norbert," she countered. "Much more professional sounding."

"Too old-fashioned."

"Actually, I like the name Parker," Nora said. "For a girl or a boy."

"A unisex name? No way! What's your mother's name?"

"Chastity." She wouldn't wish that on a baby.

Apparently, neither would he. "How about your father's?"

That reminded her that her dad still hadn't called or sent a birthday card. One year he hadn't remembered until the Fourth of July. She tried not to feel hurt. After all, she understood that he got preoccupied with work. "Dwight. What about yours?"

"It was Arthur, but we weren't close." Leo's tone darkened.

While she wasn't sure she'd want to name a baby after either of their fathers, the residual anger in his tone troubled her. "When did he die?"

"Eight years ago. He had a stroke my senior year in college." Leo's jaw twitched, and for a moment she expected him to change the subject. Instead, he said, "He never approved of me."

"Because you weren't as good a student as your brother?" She'd picked up that much from him.

"I doubt I could have pleased him no matter how hard I tried, so of course I didn't try at all," Leo conceded. "He was impatient and irritable with the whole family but especially me. He only showed his affable side in public. He loved the attention—presiding as mayor, presenting cases in court or speaking at some event. It was like he wanted us to be either perfect or invisible."

"How awful." Nora couldn't imagine having a father like that. Then, to her surprise, she realized she *could* imagine being married to someone like him. "I got a taste of that with Reese. He wanted this idealized woman who'd reflect well on him. Any variation, like gaining ten pounds or aging a few years, and he was off to greener pastures."

Leo chuckled. "Looks like he got what he deserved with—what's her name?—India?"

"Persia."

"Knew it was on that continent somewhere." His mood sobered again. "I get that feeling at work these days."

"What feeling?"

"That I'm damned if I do and damned if I don't," he said.

She tightened her arms around him, enjoying the end-of-day masculine scent infusing his shirt. "Because you've been trying so hard to make detective and you got smacked down about the Hightowers?"

She felt his nod against the top of her head. "Today, I kept second-guessing myself. But...well, can't talk about it, I'm afraid."

Her concerns flooded back. Darn, just when she was

feeling comfortable. "Did you reach Ted? I heard he lives with his mother."

"Can't comment." Leo studied the arrangement on the coffee table, which he'd nearly brushed with his foot. "Those are beautiful flowers. For your birthday?"

"No."

"Secret admirer?" Despite the light tone, she caught a hint of…could that be jealousy?

"I bought them for myself at Rose's Posies. You didn't notice them in the case?"

"The only case I noticed was the one we're investigating." Leo relaxed beneath her.

"Which you can't talk about."

"Right." Leo slid her gently onto the couch beside him. "Sorry, but my legs are falling asleep. And in case you're wondering, Theodore is out."

"I'm sorry?"

"As a baby name."

She laughed. "Got it. No unethical computer geeks, no unisex names—any other restrictions?"

Leo's palm traced the slight curve of her stomach. "If it's a boy, something strong and old-fashioned. Doesn't have to be macho. Intelligent is good."

"How about Socrates?"

He grinned. "Not that old-fashioned."

"How about Einstein?"

"Not that intelligent."

She tickled him, he tickled her back, and they play-wrestled until they remembered her delicate condition. Then they watched an action movie on TV and slept with their arms around each other.

On Sunday, Leo left early, since he had patrol duty. Lingering over a cup of tea, Nora thought how lucky she was.

She'd fallen in love with an honorable, caring man, and

she was having his baby. They could go on like this indefinitely, maybe forever. What was wrong with that? Okay, it wasn't everything she wanted, but it was more than half.

Shouldn't three-quarters of a dream be enough?

ON MONDAY, AN UNDERCURRENT of anticipation ran through the police department. From Patty, who'd heard it from Mike, Leo learned that the captain planned to make a final recommendation to the chief within the next day or so. From snatches of conversation, he also learned that the department's public information officer had decided not to return from maternity leave.

He doubted anyone would consider him for the position, and he'd decline it anyway. Dealing with the press and public might in some instances be a steppingstone to upper management, but Leo knew his own temperament. No sense taking a job he wasn't cut out for.

"Me, either," Patty told him that afternoon after Leo had shared his thoughts on the matter as they staked out an intersection on Coast Highway, where speeders had been running red lights. Even the tickets issued from overhead cameras hadn't put a dent in the dangerous behavior. "Can you see me making nice with an egomaniac like Councilman Hightower?"

"Trent would be good at it." Obviously.

"Yeah, let's hope they stick the square peg in the square hole. Or stick him in some kind of hole."

That would leave the detective position up for grabs between him and Patty. Leo considered her the clear frontrunner. This latest report wouldn't hurt, either.

On Saturday, they'd found Ted at home, ready to spill everything. He'd freely told them about referring young women to the attorney for a commission, which was legal, but he'd also uneasily admitted trying to put pressure on

Violet. Although he claimed it was for her own good, he was obviously embarrassed.

He'd been gambling online and borrowing money from shady sources, and he was scared. All the same, he'd seemed offended at the very notion that he would steal money from Mrs. Nguyen. He hadn't considered swiping a password as stealing. Amazing how naive a geek could be about the serious spread of cybercrime.

As far as who had leaked the information about Nora's patients, he'd claimed ignorance. Ted was so open about everything else that Leo honestly didn't think he knew what they were talking about. The mother, who Ted revealed had been giving him money, hadn't been home. The detective who followed up would have to talk to her and the administrator.

"One way or another, I guess we won't be partners anymore," Patty observed.

"Too bad. I hope we can still hang after work. As much as our schedules allow." Detectives worked more regular hours. They received better pay, too.

"Hey, you ever consider taking in a roommate?" she asked. "My landlord wants my apartment for his son and my lease is up, so I have to move. I mean, you've got two bedrooms."

Leo braced as an SUV appeared about to speed right through the light, but the driver hit the brakes. "Is that a bedroom? I thought it was a storage unit."

"Okay, I guess you'd rather have Blondie move in, anyway. Or are you moving in with her?"

"Nobody's moving in with anybody," he grumbled. While Nora hadn't actually mentioned the *M*-word, she'd sent a loud-and-clear message. Or was it possible she might be open to renegotiating?

"Holy cow!" Patty shouted. Right in front of them, a

pickup flew through a red light, barreling toward a Mini Cooper half its size.

At the last possible instant, the tiny car dodged out of the way. The pickup driver veered and skimmed past, not even bothering to stop.

They hit the siren and peeled out. A block later, to Leo's relief, the truck pulled over. He hated endangering lives with a vehicle chase.

The driver proved stumble-drunk, with a string of DUIs on his record. Booking him and filling out the paperwork took up the rest of their shift.

Leo was about to change into street clothes when he got a call to see the captain. Although he'd considered himself prepared to receive the news either way, his stomach tensed. It was like being called into the principal's office, he thought as he marched upstairs. He'd had that happen a few times. Okay, more than a few.

As he walked through the detective bureau, interested gazes needled his back. Just like the kids in high school. Yeah, he must be regressing.

The door to Captain Reed's office stood open. Inside, he saw no sign of the sergeant or the chief. Leo's heart sank. Definitely not a welcome-to-the-good-old-boys-club.

"You wanted to see me, sir?"

"Have a seat." The captain gestured at a chair. "Close the door, would you?"

Leo complied. On the captain's computer screen, he spotted a copy of Patty's report about Ted Chong. What was up with that?

"You and Officer Hartman appear to have nipped a crime wave in the bud," Reed said drily.

"A real desperado," Leo deadpanned.

"You both put a lot of work into that report."

"Thanks."

Reed closed the image. "What concerns me is what you *didn't* pursue."

"I beg your pardon?" Had they forgotten to dot some i's or cross some t's?

"These patients at the hospital whose information may have been stolen. The report only lists first names."

"That's all Dr. Kendall told me," Leo said.

"That would be your friend, correct?"

"Yes, sir."

"So you didn't bother to ask her for any further details?"

Where was the captain heading with this? "She cited patient confidentiality."

Reed's foot tapped the floor. He was building to something. And here it came. "So, since your partner was writing the report and getting the credit, you didn't bother to press the issue."

Leo hung on to his temper. "Once the doctor invoked confidentiality, I considered it improper to pressure her. Who got the credit had nothing to do with it."

"You're sure about that?"

In Leo's judgment, the captain was completely out of line. But arguing wasn't going to accomplish anything. "Give the promotion to Patty. She'll make a fine detective."

"I'll keep that in mind." The captain gave him a nod of dismissal.

Leo struggled to keep his expression blank as he went out. Sure enough, curious glances followed him as he made his way from the detective bureau. Well, they'd have to wait for the official results.

Maybe he should have gone and congratulated Patty on her upcoming promotion, but Leo wasn't feeling that magnanimous. So he went home and took out his foul mood on the billiard balls instead.

Chapter Nineteen

"What are you doing?"

Coffee cup in hand, Bailey plopped into a chair at Nora's table in the nearly empty hospital cafeteria. Even this late on a Monday afternoon, they were usually still seeing patients, but Nora had cleared her schedule for another long-distance staff conference with Dr. Tartikoff, and then he'd cancelled at the last minute.

Nora held up a baby-name book bristling with yellow sticky notes. "Reviewing the options. It'll be easier once I find out the sex, but I thought I'd get a jump on it."

"Didn't you already decide on Parker?"

Bailey had way too good a memory, Nora mused. "I'm not sure a unisex name is such a great idea."

"Parker isn't unisex, it's a boy's name," her nurse corrected. "But it would be cool for a girl, too."

"I suppose so." Nora took a sip of her orange tea, and discovered it had gone cold. Still tasted good, though.

Bailey plopped her feet on a chair. "It doesn't seem fair that I won't get to name mine."

Nora regarded the sprinkling of freckles across her nurse's cheeks. They'd faded during the winter, but the early April sunshine was reviving them. By midsummer, they'd be in full bloom, as she'd learned during the five years Bailey had worked for her.

"Has it really been five years?" she said aloud.

"Has what been five years?"

Nora focused on her nurse. "I think of you as being right out of nursing school, but you must be getting close to thirty."

Bailey's eyebrows shot up. "I'm twenty-eight, thank you very much."

"Are you sure you want to have a baby for your sister?" Nora blurted. "You have such mixed feelings about it."

The nurse folded her arms. "I *am* going to do this. Phyllis practically raised me. She's twelve years older than me, and in a lot of ways, she was the most stable part of my childhood."

Which wasn't saying a lot, Nora knew from having heard some of Bailey's tales of her much-married mother and absentee dad. "All the same…"

"All the same, when are *you* going to come clean?" Bailey demanded.

"About what?"

"Artificial insemination, my eye." The nurse tapped the name book. "Somebody else has a problem with unisex names, doesn't he?"

Nora didn't bother to deny it. "Yes."

"Let me guess. Daddy wears a uniform, right?"

She nodded.

"Wedding bells?"

"Unlikely." Nora refused to write them off altogether, though.

"Oh, come on. If he's so involved that he cares about the name, then…" Bailey broke off, glancing toward the cafeteria entrance. "Here comes Dr. Rayburn's secretary."

Nora was troubled to see May's eyes rimmed in red as the woman approached. "Oh, dear."

"She's headed straight toward us. What do you suppose she wants?"

Nora hadn't said a word about the apparent adoption scheme to her staff. "No telling."

"Yeah? That isn't very convincing. You sure have been keeping a lot of secrets," Bailey groused.

"You're pretty good at guessing them. But I'd appreciate if you'd leave the two of us alone for now." Nora gave her an apologetic shrug. "I'll explain later."

"You better. I hate hearing gossip about my doctor from anyone else." With a hello-and-goodbye, the nurse departed.

May Chong dropped into the vacated seat. A few days ago, she'd appeared discouraged about her son's gambling but determined to set him straight. Now, all the fight had gone out of her. Her usually shiny, straight dark hair hung lank, as if she'd finger-combed it to death, and her complexion looked sallow.

"Your service told me you were here," she said. "Dr. Kendall, I'm so sorry."

"Tell me what's happened." Nora waited tensely for an answer. Now matter how sympathetic she felt, she had to put her patients' interests first.

The secretary interlaced her fingers atop the table. "Dr. Rayburn talked to me this morning. I expected it, after Ted told me what he'd done. Hassling that girl and everything. What a stupid idea!"

"He admitted it to the police?" Nora had been wondering about the interview, since Leo couldn't discuss it with her.

"He told them he stole her password. They didn't arrest him, but he thinks they might still prosecute. These matters take a while, he said. He's been doing research on the internet, about legal things. He's a smart boy." Tears shimmered.

Nora could no longer avoid the painful question on her mind. "Did you leak my patients' information to that attorney?"

Her face flushing with shame, May nodded. "Mr. Bridger didn't know I stole the names. He pays a lot for referrals. My son is deep in debt and I already drained my savings. I thought I was helping him, and everybody. One of the couples already got a baby, didn't they?"

"Yes, but it was wrong. You can't release personal data like that."

"It was only those two women, nobody else. Now the hospital has to pay for a big audit. All that money's wasted, and there's no telling what the police will do to me and Ted." She began crying. "Dr. Sam came in and was so disappointed in me. I feel terrible. I handed Dr. Rayburn my resignation."

Instinctively, Nora cupped the woman's hand. "What will you do now?"

May sniffled. "My brother needs a secretary for his car dealership in Santa Ana. I called and he said he'd hire me. Ted, too, if he's willing to sell cars. Assuming we don't go to jail."

"Sell cars? That's hardly his field," Nora observed.

"Who would trust him around their computers?"

"I suppose that's true." Before he could even begin to recover his reputation and his career, though, Ted had to deal with his addiction. "Has he contacted Gamblers Anonymous?"

"Yes. There's a chapter that meets a few miles from here. We'll go together. Dr. Rayburn says I was enabling him, that if I didn't keep bailing him out, maybe he'd have quit by now. I guess I need to change, too." From her purse, May drew a wad of tissues and blew her nose.

Nora sat with her a while longer. She hated seeing the secretary leave her job, but it was unavoidable.

"Please stay in touch," Nora told her. "Let me know if there's anything I can do."

"I will. I appreciate the offer."

After May left, Nora supposed she should tell Leo about the secretary's resignation. Since he should be off duty by now, she pressed his number in her cell. It went to voice mail. She clicked off without leaving a message.

Maybe he and Patty had gone to catch a movie and he'd turned off the phone. She decided to try later.

After an early dinner, Nora called and got voice mail again. A sudden fear hit her—what if he'd been injured on the job?

Her hands went cold. She hadn't seriously considered how risky Leo's job was, perhaps because he always seemed so strong and in control. But even in a town as quiet as Safe Harbor, a car chase could get out of hand, or a gang from L.A. could try to pull off a robbery.

Maybe he'd been taken to one of the hospitals in the area. She could check with emergency rooms or the police dispatcher. No, a better source would be Tony, his next of kin.

You're overreacting. Most likely, she'd accomplish nothing except to make a complete fool of herself. He was probably fine.

Still, she didn't intend to sit around stewing. On impulse, Nora picked up the baby-name book, jotted a note in case no one answered the bell and drove to Leo's house.

The fading light revealed considerable improvement since the last time she'd been here. The shutters had been repainted and the lawn had filled in where weeds used to dominate.

She was starting up the walk when a rackety noise on

the sidewalk drew her attention. A long-haired guy in jeans and sweatshirt came shooting along on a skateboard, spun a wheelie and hopped off.

"So, hey." Not a guy, but Patty.

"Hi." Nora palmed the book, trying to keep the title out of sight. "Any idea if Leo's home?"

"Must be. Or else he's got mice with long toenails." The other woman jerked her head toward the house. Then Nora heard it, too—the *clack-clack* of billiard balls. Leo must be hitting them hard.

"Sounds like he's mad."

"Yeah, it does." The blonde officer stuck the board under her arm. "I've been circling, trying to work up the nerve to find out what happened with the captain. He kind of got called on the carpet."

"About what?"

"Mike—Detective Mike Aaron—thinks it's about your patients. Mike doesn't exactly bug the captain's office but he's got ears like a hawk."

"He has to track them down?" Nora asked in dismay. While she and the hospital would inform both families that their information had been compromised so they could put security alerts on their credit accounts, this went way beyond that. Being questioned by the police would upset them.

It might also lead to lawsuits. What a mess.

"I don't see how he can, with only first names. But there was some kind of scene in the captain's office—people couldn't hear it, but they could see the body language."

"Bad, huh?"

Patty scuffed the sidewalk. "Half the department thinks I deliberately wrote the report in a way that made Leo look bad. Like I stabbed him in the back to get the promotion. He has to realize it's not true, but I don't think he feels like talking to me. I hate office politics."

"Me, too." Nora felt awful about the entire situation. "Is he in trouble? Will this business about my patients cost him the promotion?"

"It might if the captain doesn't think he was dedicated enough, that he didn't push you because the two of you are involved," the other woman said.

This was terrible. Even though Nora would never have revealed her patients' names no matter who had questioned her, the captain apparently assumed otherwise.

Patty tilted her head. "What's with all the sticky notes?"

To her dismay, Nora realized the book had slipped into view. *Think fast.* "Something we were discussing. I'll leave it for him." She tried to tuck the book out of sight.

Too late. "Baby names. Oh!"

Great. Nora had spilled their secret. "Listen, this has to be kept completely private."

Patty raised her hands. "They won't hear it from me. Honest. I do tend to talk too much but I've had it with gossip."

The front door opened. "Nora, come in." Leo gave a cool nod in Patty's direction, and his partner hung back. As the door closed behind Nora, she heard the skateboard rumble away. It was a lonely sound.

She put her arms around Leo. "I'm sorry things blew up at work. Maybe if I hadn't gotten you involved in the counseling center, none of this would have happened."

He kissed the top of her head. "I got myself involved. Besides, you're the best thing I've got going right now." Before she could react, he added, "Don't take that as anything too heavy, okay?"

"I'm just glad you aren't lying in intensive care somewhere or being rushed into surgery," Nora said. "It scared me when you didn't answer your phone." *And I realized no one would call me because I'm not your next of kin.* But he had enough on his mind without hearing that.

He stepped back. "I didn't mean to frighten you."

"I shouldn't let my imagination run away with me." The feel of the book in her hand reminded her of her excuse for visiting. "I thought you might enjoy looking through this."

"What is it?" Leo examined the cover. "There's a book about names?"

"More than onc." At the local bookstore, Nora had been impressed by the section on babies.

Leaning against the wall, he flipped through it. Didn't invite her to sit down or have a drink, but considering how upset he must be at losing his promotion, simply acting civil was likely a strain.

Leo looked up. "You only marked boys' names. Are you telling me something?"

Such an indirect tactic would never have occurred to her. "I didn't get around to the girls' names yet."

He examined a page bristling with tiny yellow stick-ons. "Lincoln. Logan. Mortimer. You're kidding about that one, right?"

"I picked Mortimer?" Nora leaned closer. Leo had been eating potato chips, she gathered from the salty potato scent, and wondered if there were any left. "The paper slipped. Micah, that's what I marked."

"Sure are a lot of names." Leo closed the book without further discussion. "I'll look through this later."

She recognized her cue to leave but she couldn't yet. He needed her support. And she needed simply to be near him. "Patty says you stood up to the captain. What's that mean?"

"It means maybe I don't respect him as much as I thought," Leo returned grimly.

She had no idea how a police department worked. Could this put a permanent black mark on his record? "There'll be other advancement opportunities, won't there?"

"Eventually. It's a small department." Waning daylight through the front window cast shadows across his face. "Originally, I thought I'd rather work for a big or even medium-sized department. But this is my community and I care about it. At least, that was the rationale when I took the job."

It hadn't occurred to Nora that he might go elsewhere. "You'd consider leaving?"

"I might see what positions are available." He didn't sound thrilled about the idea.

"You stood up to him for me." Strange how she could feel gratified and regretful at the same time.

"I did it because it was the right thing," Leo corrected.

That reminded her of the conversation at the cafeteria. "Oh. I meant to tell you. May came to see me. She admits stealing information to make the referrals, and she resigned."

"What's the hospital going to do?"

"An audit, as you suggested," Nora said.

"What else did she say?"

Whatever she told him would probably make its way into some report or other, but Nora didn't see any reason to hold back. "May insists there were no other patients affected, just those two. Frankly, I believe her. She imagined she was doing everybody a favor."

"Guess that's where her son got his mixed-up ideas." Leo shifted his stance restlessly.

"Is he going to be prosecuted?"

"That will be up to the district attorney," he muttered. Wound tight, he was clearly sticking to his word about not discussing the case.

"Go whack some more billiard balls." Nora touched his shoulder lightly. "I'll talk to you later."

"Later," he echoed, and let her out.

Driving away, Nora recalled his precious words. *"You're the best thing I've got going right now."* The statement warmed her.

If only he would quit backing away. If only she could be sure of what was in his heart.

If only she weren't afraid that events might be pushing them toward a tipping point, beyond which they'd be drawn further and further apart until there was nothing left.

LEAFING THROUGH THE BABY book that night, Leo discovered he was sounding out the possibilities with Franco. Sean Franco. Stewart Franco. Wouldn't Nora more likely use Kendall? From a practical standpoint, it made sense for the child and mother to share the same surname. But something about the prospect bothered him.

For a distraction, he read the girls' section. Juliet was pretty, and a sweet counterpoint to the hard *K* sounds in Kendall and Franco. He wondered if Nora had considered that aspect when she suggested Parker.

Finally he chucked the book onto his bedside table and went to sleep.

On Tuesday, the atmosphere in the patrol car was strained. A couple of times, he caught Patty studying pregnant women on the street and glancing at him as if about to ask a question. Wonderful. Obviously she'd put the less-than-subtle clues together from the baby-name book.

He wasn't in the mood to discuss his private business with her. Or anyone connected with work.

Patty asked to be dropped off at the station at noon, supposedly to finish up a few tasks for Mike. Leo figured she'd been asked to schmooze with the higher-ups. All those congratulations and the celebrating would go down a lot easier while he was in the field. For him, too.

"Good luck," he said as she got out.

"Later."

He resumed patrolling the quiet streets of Safe Harbor. Not being in the mood for paperwork, he let a stop-sign-running mom off with a warning. Anyway, you had to sympathize with the distractions posed by a crying baby and a shrieking toddler.

At shift change, he expected to pick up a lot of undercurrents among the other officers, but the only obvious development concerned Trent Horner, who was grinning from ear to ear. He'd been chosen as the replacement for the public information officer who was not returning from maternity leave.

"You deserve it." Leo didn't have to feign enthusiasm as he high-fived the guy. "Perfect job for you."

"I'm drawing up proposals right now." Trent launched into a description of how he planned to expand the city's Neighborhood Watch program and institute programs for senior citizens and high school students to learn more about the mission, policies and day-to-day operations of the department.

Leo was impressed. Some of the ideas might seem like fluff, but others could actually help curb crime.

A records clerk and a dispatcher, both single ladies who apparently liked their men blond and shiny, soon joined Trent's audience. Leo was glad to slip away.

He changed into street clothes, tensing whenever someone entered the locker room. Things were in the wind today, and he assumed he'd get a summons to the captain's office to receive his share of bad news.

The summons came, all right. He was on his way out

when the chief's secretary stopped him. "Leo? Chief Walters would like to see you in his office," she said.

His gut knotted. Why was the chief involved? As far as Leo was concerned, he hadn't committed any major screwups. But the captain might see it differently.

This time, walking through the station, he definitely caught a buzz and a lot of sideways glances. The sooner he got this over with, the better.

Chapter Twenty

Nora felt as if she wore a path between the hospital and the medical building on Tuesday. Three deliveries had to be squeezed between patient appointments, and even though her staff allowed a bit of wiggle room in her schedule, she got plenty of exercise jogging to and fro.

Exercise was good for her baby, but later on she would have to slow down. It occurred to her that performing deliveries and surgery might get awkward when she stuck out to there, both in terms of her stance and of her stamina. On the other hand, staff members catered to surgeons. All you had to do was mention you were hungry or thirsty, and someone fetched refreshments. Too bad that didn't happen everywhere she went!

During her spare moments at the hospital, she found the nurses humming with the news about May's resignation. In the afternoon, Samantha stopped by as Nora was leaving Labor and Delivery to apologize for not keeping closer tabs on the counseling center.

"It's not as if you could have foreseen what Ted was up to," Nora said as they paused in front of the hospital nursery. She enjoyed stopping here to see the infants she'd delivered.

"No, but I basically left you to fend for yourself, and

that's not right," the tall pediatrician replied. "I appreciate how you and Leo helped Suzy and her boyfriend."

"I had no idea there'd be so much drama in doing a little volunteer work." Nora studied the tiny faces of the infants, some sleeping, some gazing about contentedly. Delicate hands waved, little bodies wiggled and here and there a cry—muted by the glass—summoned a soothing nurse.

How amazing that in another seven months, one of those would be hers.

"Everything in life's full of drama, isn't it?" Sam replied. "Hope to see you there again." With a wave, she was off.

As Nora lingered for another delicious moment, a young woman in a hospital gown strolled up, holding the arm of her beaming husband. They peered through the observation window, exclaiming over their child.

"His ears are just like my brother's," observed the woman.

"They're exactly like my dad's," her husband teased.

"No way! Your dad has weird ears." The new mom poked him in the side.

"So does your brother." He caught her hand. "Come to think of it, so do you."

They both dissolved into laughter.

Envy at their closeness burned into Nora. Where would Leo be in seven months? Here with her? Or somewhere else, perhaps *with* someone else?

She turned away quickly. A few steps farther, her phone vibrated, and the readout identified the caller as her father.

"Hi, Dad." She strolled into the nearest physicians' lounge. "Is everything all right?"

"Yes, except for the fact that I'm late for your birthday again." Dwight Halvorsen's voice sounded drier than ever now that he'd reached his mid-sixties.

"That's become a tradition." She took a comfortable chair.

"I'm sending you a present," he said. "The newly revised version of my biology textbook. It's dedicated to you."

"To me?" Nora hadn't expected that. "Thanks, Dad. That's a wonderful birthday present."

"Good!" He sounded relieved. "I never know what to buy you."

"I'm kind of old for presents, anyway."

"You're never too old for presents," her father said cheerily. "Also, I have some news."

"Really?" Normally, little changed in her father's world. Until his retirement, he'd taught and worked in his lab, and during the past year, he'd spent his time updating the textbook.

"Now that I'm done shepherding all those revisions into print, I've decided to take on a new challenge. I'm going to spend the fall semester in Tucson, teaching a seminar and working on a research project at the University of Arizona."

"Congratulations!"

"Retirement doesn't suit me. I have too much drive."

"Good! You'll be happier if you stay active."

As they discussed his plans for next fall, Nora reflected on how comfortably the two of them talked about work. They'd always shared a love of biology. Anything personal was another matter. Throughout her divorce, she'd spared her father the painful details, deliberately giving the impression that she and Reese had parted amicably.

Well, she could hardly keep her pregnancy secret. And she had no idea how to soft-pedal the fact that she was having this baby alone.

"Dad?"

He broke off a description of his recent visit to Biosphere

2, the site near Tucson of some innovative biological experiments. "What is it, honey?"

"I'm pregnant."

"I'm going to be a grandfather?" His voice filled with joy. "When are you due? Can I come out for the delivery?"

She hadn't expected that reaction. Awkwardly phrased questions and a stilted attempt at reassurance, perhaps. But not this rush of excitement.

"Of course. I'm due in November." Then everything spilled out. How much she'd wanted a baby during her marriage and how devastated she'd been by Reese's betrayal. Meeting Leo, getting pregnant, trying to figure out their roles.

Her father listened patiently. When she wound down, he said, "Do you love him?"

Could this be her father asking such an intimate thing? Amazing. "Yes," Nora said.

"More than you loved Reese?"

"Yes," she said again, without hesitation. "Why do you ask?"

"I never much liked that man," her dad said. "Too oily. But if you were happy, I was happy."

"You didn't tell me that!" She'd had no idea her father didn't care for Reese.

"We never talk about these things," he said. "But you're grown now. I don't have to protect you from my feelings."

"Protect me? I thought I was protecting you!"

"What on earth gave you that idea?" The pitch of his voice arched with astonishment, like a raised eyebrow.

"I was always so awkward and clumsy," Nora said. "In my love life, I mean. I didn't want to embarrass you."

"Embarrass me? I was afraid you'd pick up on how tone-deaf I am about relationships. I couldn't believe your mother married me and put up with my bumbling manners. The way I forget birthdays and holidays, and wear clothes till they fall apart."

"That's what I'm like, too. Well, not the part about my clothes, but I had zero fashion sense before I married Reese." His tutelage on how to dress for success was one of the few positives she'd retained from her marriage. "I was this complete social disaster."

"You're the most beautiful, graceful woman in the world! Any man who doesn't appreciate that doesn't deserve you."

She wished her dad was right here instead of a couple of hours' drive away in Santa Barbara, so she could hug him. "That's the sweetest thing you ever said to me, Dad."

"I wish I'd said it years ago."

"I love you."

"That goes double for me. The day you were born was the most wonderful day of my life." Impishly, he added, "I'm expecting a certain day in November to be a close second, though."

They talked awhile longer about his plans to rent out the house and find a place in Tucson. Afterward Nora took a much-needed trip to the ladies' room. Washing her hands, she studied her face in the mirror.

Classic oval. Green eyes. Blond hair tucked into a practical bun. How many times over the years had people told her she was beautiful? She'd never felt that way, though. Now, crinkles formed at the edges of her mouth and pregnancy had given her a slight puffiness.

To Reese, she probably looked past her prime. But she didn't see herself through Reese's eyes anymore.

Nora liked the wrinkles, because she'd earned them during years of helping other people. She liked her eyes, too. Not because of their color or shape but because they served their function well—to examine patients, to observe friends, to enjoy the sight of babies in the nursery.

As for her body, so what if it had a tendency to put on weight? Her hands were steady in surgery, and her legs carried her between her office and the hospital. Most important, her womb held a healthy baby.

Whether she was beautiful or plain, slender or stocky, young or coasting toward middle age no longer mattered. For the first time in her life, Nora truly liked what she saw in the mirror.

THE CHIEF'S OFFICE OCCUPIED a large corner of the second floor, in the front of the police station. It was twice as large as the captain's, with a conference table and a view of the Civic Center complex.

As he entered, Leo saw three other men present: Chief Jon Walters, a fifty-something man with cropped sandy hair, pale eyes and military bearing; Captain Reed and Sergeant Hough. Receiving a nod from the chief, Leo took the only vacant seat in a semicircle around the large desk.

"Your name seems to come up frequently these days." The chief studied him levelly. Walters never tried to act chummy with the officers, but was both fair and reasonably friendly. "As you may have heard, Roy Hightower called to withdraw his earlier complaint. In fact, he seems impressed with you."

"Thank you, sir." Leo knew he hadn't been summoned here for that, so he waited for whatever came next.

The chief lifted a sheet of stationery. Even at this angle, Leo recognized the Safe Harbor Medical Center letterhead. "I received a letter from Dr. Samantha Forrest complimenting your volunteer work at the Edward Serra counseling center. It seems you went above and beyond in assisting a young man through a crisis."

"He's a good kid," Leo said carefully. "I was glad to help." From outside, he heard the *vroom* of a motorcycle circling the building, but otherwise the soundproofing in here was impressive.

"One more recommendation." The chief folded his hands on the desk. "Officer Hartman credits you with identifying the suspect in the situation involving Councilman Hightower's son. She says you broke the case by developing community contacts."

Patty could easily have stayed silent and received the credit. After all, she'd written the report, and Leo had no doubt that Mike Aaron had spoken up strongly on her behalf. "We worked on it as a team."

"He may not have heard the resolution," Captain Reed put in. "After Chong admitted harassing the young woman, he apologized to the Nguyen family and offered to make amends by spending four weekends delivering flowers. They've requested that we drop any charges. The D.A. has the final decision, but I'm sure he'll take that into consideration."

"No other data was stolen from the computers?" Leo asked.

"The counseling center and the hospital are still determining that," the chief said. "They seem optimistic. Oh, and one more thing. Congratulations. You'll make a great detective."

For a moment, Leo didn't move, because he wasn't sure what he'd heard. Then the chief came around the desk with his hand extended. Leo scrambled to his feet and shook it.

The captain and sergeant added their congratulations, with handshakes all around. In a daze, Leo thanked them all. Questions bubbled in his brain but he held them in check. No sense spoiling the moment merely to satisfy his curiosity.

"I imagine you've heard that Officer Horner is our new public information officer," the chief added.

"Yes. He'll do a great job." *What about Patty?* It seemed impolitic to ask, however, so Leo hung on to his patience.

"Glad to see you moving up. You deserve this," the chief said.

"Thank you, sir."

Out in the hallway, Hough disappeared for some task of his own. "Mike will help you with the transition, starting tomorrow," the captain said as the two of them walked toward the detective bureau.

Leo was still trying to absorb the fact that he'd received the promotion. At least now he might ask the question foremost on his mind. "What about Patty?"

"She's been informed of our choice. She seemed pleased." Reed didn't elaborate. Might as well ask about another matter, as well.

"What was all that about pressuring Dr. Kendall? Some kind of test?"

Reed gave him a wry smile. "The reason I decided to assess the three of you is that I had certain concerns about each of you and I wanted to see how they'd play out."

"If you don't mind my asking, what was your concern about me?" Leo kept his voice too low to be overheard by anyone passing by.

"Anger issues," the captain said. "I figured if I pushed hard enough, you might blow."

"So that's what you were doing." Leo didn't like to think how close he'd come to losing his temper.

"That's nothing compared to how attorneys will push you in court. There'll be a strong temptation to use sarcasm or let your resentment show, but it's all a game to them. You win by denying them a reaction."

"Thank you, sir."

"I have a feeling I'm just telling you what you already know."

"Never hurts to hear it again."

At the entrance to the bureau, Leo noticed that every desk seemed occupied for a change. No doubt word had spread that promotions were on the line this afternoon. Although he caught a number of sideways glances, no one reacted overtly as he and Reed crossed the large room. Then Leo spotted Patty standing by Mike's desk.

Her gaze met his. And she came rushing over, grinning. "You son of a gun, way to go!" She gave him a whack on the shoulder and a big handshake.

The room erupted with movement. Now that the ice had been broken and the promotion revealed, Leo was engulfed with congratulations and offers to meet for a beer after work at the Corner Tavern. He accepted with pleasure.

Half an hour later, he finally got a moment alone with Patty in the parking lot. "Thanks for giving me credit." He studied her plain, honest face with its stubborn square jaw. "Are you sure you're okay with this?"

"Yeah. I'm pleased, actually." She shrugged. "I'm not saying I'd have turned it down, but Mike was pushing a little too hard in my corner. It wasn't fair, so I spoke up. Anyway, the captain wouldn't have given it to me."

Leo remembered Reed's concerns. He hadn't mentioned specifics about the other candidates, of course. "Why not?"

"He said I have potential but I don't guard my tongue enough. He was worried about what I might say in court. And he's right." She cleared her throat. "Now that it's over, Mike offered me a job with his detective agency, like we figured. I said yes."

"I hope you aren't leaving because of me." It meant a lot to Leo to keep his former partner as a friend.

"No, and I'm not saying anything officially until next week. I don't want to rain on your parade."

"I hate to see you go." That was putting it mildly.

"Hey, it's not like I'm moving away. The truth is, being a P.I. sounds like an adventure. I can set my own hours and, yeah, there'll be boring assignments, and there'll still be paperwork, but it's less bureaucratic." Patty glanced over as a black-and-white pulled into the lot. "I'm going to miss patrolling with you."

"Me, too."

"I'm still invited over to play pool, though, right?"

"Anytime."

"See you at the Tavern."

In his car, Leo dialed the person he most wanted to share this news with. He missed her and wanted to make up for how short he'd been with her yesterday.

He'd be earning more money now. Still working long hours as the caseload required, but not the rotating shifts that played havoc with his body clock and his personal life. That meant they could spend more time together.

He'd like that. A lot. This waking up alone got old. And while he wasn't looking forward to sleepless nights with a crying baby, he'd gladly endure them to experience close, loving moments with little Einstein/Socrates.

And, especially, close, loving moments with Nora.

When she answered, the warm tone of her voice felt like a caress. "I got it!" he said, and proceeded to fill her in on the afternoon's events.

"That's wonderful." She sounded thrilled. "Want to come over for dinner and celebrate? I don't promise to cook but I can pick up some outstanding Italian food."

He laughed. "Great. I promised to meet a few colleagues for a beer. Is seven too late?"

"I have a few errands to run myself," she said. "Seven will be perfect."

Errands. That reminded him. On his way over, he'd stop at Rose's Posies and pick up a bouquet. Nora ought to enjoy that.

Too bad he couldn't ply her with wine. One way or another, he had to persuade her to let him stay at her place for more than just the occasional overnight visit. Moving in together ought to suit them both. They could still keep it light, still stay friends.

After what had happened today, Leo was almost certain he had luck on his side.

Chapter Twenty-One

On her way home, Nora stopped by The Baby Bump to buy a couple of maternity outfits. She chose trim slacks with expandable tummies; cleverly designed tops that could be unsnapped for nursing; and a flattering pink dress with a scooped neck.

She deserved pretty clothes. And she intended to enjoy every moment of this pregnancy—those moments when she wasn't upchucking or soaking her feet.

At Papa Giovanni's, she placed an order for two pasta dishes, plus garlic bread and salad. With twenty minutes to wait, she wandered next door to gaze in the window of Jewels by Jacques. Why not treat herself to a pair of earrings, as well?

But it wasn't the earrings that caught her attention. It was a bearded man and a graying woman inside the store. Although they must be in their sixties, they were beaming like kids as the woman held out her left hand to admire an engagement ring. Even through the glass, Nora could see the diamond sparkle, or imagined she could.

A jolt of pain stabbed her heart. If only she and Leo were able to share their future like this couple. If only her handsome, dashing police officer loved her without reservation.

He was capable of deep emotion, of loving his child and,

she felt certain, of committing himself to a woman, too. *Just not you. He likes you well enough for now, but you'll never be the woman of his dreams.*

She recognized that small internal voice. It had told her many times over the years as she gazed into the mirror that she was awkward. Geeky. Not nearly as sexy as guys expected.

It hadn't believed a sophisticated man like Reese could fall for her, and had accepted, with a kind of embarrassment, that she'd lost him to a younger, more glamorous woman.

Maybe it was time for that voice to shut up.

Leo arrived at Nora's condo with a bottle of sparkling grape juice and an African violet, purple blooms peeking past glossy green leaves. He'd chosen a plant rather than cut flowers so she could enjoy it for a long time. Rose had assured him it was safe to grow around children.

Nora accepted the plant with obvious delight, her thumb caressing the velvety leaves. "They feel so soft, but I'm not sure whether they like being touched."

"If they don't, they're very stupid plants." He ran a thumb across her smooth cheek. "Now, humans, on the other hand…" He traced the arch of her neck and the scoop of her green top down to the swell of her breasts. He couldn't think that way. Except for light cuddling, she was off-limits.

Reluctantly, Leo drew back. "I'd better behave."

"Only temporarily," Nora assured him.

"In this case, temporary feels like forever," he admitted.

"At least I can satisfy one of your appetites. Come eat." She led him to the dining area, and through the sliding doors to the balcony he heard the relaxing ebb and flow of the surf. After the raucous jukebox and blaring TV at the tavern, his whole body sighed with relief.

Nora had set the table with bright blue plates and crystal glasses. Linen napkins and gleaming silverware, too. "Now we can have our own celebration," she told him. "I hope you had fun with your friends."

"Absolutely." His coworkers had acted genuinely pleased with his promotion. Bill and George had said privately that they were glad to see good solid police work win out over currying favor. He presumed they were referring to Trent.

"So being involved with me didn't hurt you?" She produced blue-and-white bowls full of pasta and salad.

"No, as it turned out." While they ate, Leo filled her in on what the captain had said. Retelling the story, he enjoyed watching her reaction to each small revelation. It gave him a chance to enjoy the experience all over again, without the pressure and anxiety of the first go-round.

He relished this kind of dinner-table conversation. There were none of the cold silences or snide remarks that had marked his parents' interaction during his childhood dinners. If only they could capture and hold this tender relationship. Never let it deteriorate. Never let it go stale.

He gladly found room for dessert, a rich chocolate torte. Nora had a thin slice. "I don't want to gain too much weight during my pregnancy," she explained. "But I refuse to deny myself entirely."

"You shouldn't deny yourself at all," Leo said.

"I suppose not." Across from him, she toyed with her fork and scraped the last few crumbs off her plate.

"Something on your mind?" Leo didn't understand why she seemed nervous.

She flashed him a startled look. "Oh! I have a gift for you."

A gift? "You bought dinner. That's plenty."

"This is different." She bolted from the table. Definitely nervous. About what?

He kind of hoped she would return with a new ultrasound photo. Learning the sex of the baby would cap an already memorable day. But she came back with a small velvet jeweler's box in her palm.

A tiepin? Cuff links? He didn't need any of that stuff, but he appreciated the thought. "Thanks." With a mystified smile, Leo accepted the box and pried it open.

A thick gold band, etched with a geometric design, gleamed against a black background. Subtle and masculine. He liked it, but…"Is this a wedding ring?"

He lifted his gaze to find her watching him anxiously. "This is the part I'm not sure about," Nora said. "Whether to get down on my knees. If I do that, you might have to haul me up afterward."

"You're proposing?" Instantly, he felt like an idiot. That was pretty obvious.

"Well, I *am* older than you, so I figured I should take the lead." Nora hovered nearby, still on her feet. "I realized I have a tendency to protect men emotionally, and how better can I protect you than by being your wife?"

What an odd reason to get married. Besides… "It's *my* job to protect *you*. And the baby." Reaching for her arm, Leo drew her onto his lap. That required a bit of angling and adjusting, but soon she was right where he wanted her. "I was going to suggest we move in together. Preferably here. How about it?"

"Leo." A pucker formed between her eyebrows. "You've gotten stuck in your thinking. We're having a baby. I love you. We stand side by side even when things go wrong. I need to know we'll always be here for each other, and our child deserves that security, too."

"Of course I'll always be here for you. I love you." He tightened his grip around her.

"Think about it, okay?" Nora kissed his temple. "You don't have to give me an answer right now."

"All right." If he said no to marriage, would she still say yes to him moving in? He had a feeling she wouldn't. That made no sense. They were friends, as well as lovers. They belonged...

Together.

Leo didn't know any other couple where the woman had proposed. But then, they were different from other couples in a lot of ways.

So what makes you think your marriage will be like anyone else's, either?

He remembered when Ralph asked if he'd been in love. Leo had answered truthfully that he'd never been involved with a woman who couldn't be replaced.

Until now.

He'd never find anyone else like Nora. And he didn't want to.

"Okay. Yes," Leo said. "I'll marry you, on one condition."

She took a breath before responding. "What's that?"

"You have to let me move in with you."

Nora burst out laughing. "That's a tough one. Yes."

"And promise that we'll always talk things over. That we won't get angry and clam up, or assign blame or try to impose preconceived roles. That we'll stay like this. Best friends." Leo hadn't intended to deliver a speech, but there it was.

"Yes, yes, yes," Nora said, and kissed his jaw.

Instead of feeling trapped, he felt his heart expand. They were going to move through life, supporting and loving each other. "Wow," Leo said, "this is bigger than I expected."

"What do you mean?"

"I feel like I got promoted all over again." From boyfriend

to husband. Even the word *marriage*, which for so long had clanged like a prison door, now chimed merrily.

Wedding bells. He was actually looking forward to them.

THEY SAT OUTSIDE ON THE patio, listening to the waves. Stars sparkled in the night sky, and below the bluffs, moonlight glimmered off the ocean. Nora had never believed she could feel so happy.

There were endless details to discuss on this glorious evening when their commitment was as fresh as a newborn baby. Leo was going to rent his house to Patty and buy a car big enough to carry a family, he said, although Nora protested that she'd miss that little red zinger. She promised to make room in her study for his pool table, but after considering the logistics, he decided to leave it where it was.

They snuggled beneath a fleece blanket. Faces cold, bodies warm. Nora wondered if, seen from a distance, they emitted a subtle glow. Or maybe not so subtle.

"Big wedding or small?" Leo asked.

She burrowed deeper into him. "I already had a big wedding. It didn't take. But I do want a church full of flowers."

"Suits me."

It struck her that her father might enjoy walking her down the aisle. He'd ducked that duty the last time, with some excuse or other. Now she understood why—his dislike of Reese. This time, it would be wonderful to share her happiness with him.

Big or small, luxurious or simple, it didn't matter. As long as she had Leo waiting for her by the altar, Dr. Nora Kendall was definitely in the mood for a wedding.

* * * * *

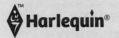

Harlequin®

American ★ *Romance*®

COMING NEXT MONTH

Available March 8, 2011

#1345 THE COMEBACK COWBOY
American Romance's Men of the West
Cathy McDavid

#1346 THE DOCTOR'S FOREVER FAMILY
Forever, Texas
Marie Ferrarella

#1347 SECOND CHANCE DAD
Fatherhood
Pamela Stone

#1348 THE RELUCTANT BRIDE
Anne Marie Duquette

REQUEST YOUR FREE BOOKS!
2 FREE NOVELS PLUS 2 FREE GIFTS!

 Harlequin®

 American ★ Romance®

LOVE, HOME & HAPPINESS

USA TODAY *bestselling author Lynne Graham*
is back with a thrilling new trilogy
SECRETLY PREGNANT, CONVENIENTLY WED

Three heroines must marry alpha males to keep
their dreams…but Alejandro, Angelo and Cesario
are not about to be tamed!

Book 1—JEMIMA'S SECRET
Available March 2011 from Harlequin Presents®.

JEMIMA yanked open a drawer in the sideboard to find Alfie's birth certificate. Her son was her husband's child. It was a question of telling the truth whether she liked it or not. She extended the certificate to Alejandro.

"This has to be nonsense," Alejandro asserted.

"Well, if you can find some other way of explaining how I managed to give birth by that date and Alfie not be yours, I'd like to hear it," Jemima challenged.

Alejandro glanced up, golden eyes bright as blades and as dangerous. "All this proves is that you must still have been pregnant when you walked out on our marriage. It does not automatically follow that the child is mine."

"'I know it doesn't suit you to hear this news now and I really didn't want to tell you. But I can't lie to you about it. Someday Alfie may want to look you up and get acquainted."

"If what you have just told me is the truth, if that little boy does prove to be mine, it was vindictive and extremely selfish of you to leave me in ignorance!"

Jemima paled. "When I left you, I had no idea that I was still pregnant."

"Two years is a long period of time, yet you made no attempt to inform me that I might be a father. I will want DNA tests to confirm your claim before I make any decision about what I want to do."

"Do as you like," she told him curtly. "*I* know who Alfie's father is and there has never been any doubt of his identity."

"I will make arrangements for the tests to be carried out and I will see you again when the result is available," Alejandro drawled with lashings of dark Spanish masculine reserve.

"I'll contact a solicitor and start the divorce," Jemima proffered in turn.

Alejandro's eyes narrowed in a piercing scrutiny that made her uncomfortable. "It would be foolish to do anything before we have that DNA result."

"I disagree," Jemima flashed back. "I should have applied for a divorce the minute I left you!"

Alejandro quirked an ebony brow. "And why didn't you?"

Jemima dealt him a fulminating glance but said nothing, merely moving past him to open her front door in a blunt invitation for him to leave.

"I'll be in touch," he delivered on the doorstep.

What is Alejandro's next move? Perhaps rekindling their marriage is the only solution! But will Jemima agree?

Find out in Lynne Graham's
exciting new romance
JEMIMA'S SECRET

Available March 2011
from Harlequin Presents®.

Start your Best Body today with these top 3 nutrition tips!

1. **SHOP THE PERIMETER OF THE GROCERY STORE:** The good stuff—fruits, veggies, lean proteins and dairy—always line the outer edges of the store. When you veer into the center aisles, you enter the temptation zone, where the unhealthy foods live.

2. **WATCH PORTION SIZES:** Most portion sizes in restaurants are nearly twice the size of a true serving and at home, it's easy to "clean your plate." Use these easy serving guidelines:
   - Protein: the palm of your hand
   - Grains or Fruit: a cup of your hand
   - Veggies: the palm of two open hands

3. **USE THE RAINBOW RULE FOR PRODUCE:** Your produce drawers should be filled with every color of fruits and vegetables. The greater the variety, the more vitamins and other nutrients you add to your diet.

Find these and many more helpful tips in

YOUR BEST BODY NOW

by

TOSCA RENO

WITH STACY BAKER

Bestselling Author of
THE EAT-CLEAN DIET

Available wherever books are sold!

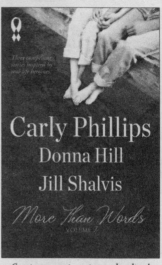